But That's Another Story

But That's Another Story

Famous Authors Introduce Popular Genres

EDITED BY SANDY ASHER

WALKER AND COMPANY   NEW YORK

First published in the United States of America in 1996
by Walker Publishing Company, Inc.

Published simultaneously in Canada by Thomas Allen & Son Canada,
Limited, Markham, Ontario

Library of Congress Cataloging-in-Publication Data
But that's another story: famous authors introduce popular genres/
    edited by Sandy Asher.
        Contents: Flying away/Angela Johnson—Alligator mystique/
    Barbara Robinson—A time to stand up/Elaine Marie Alphin—
    Echoes down the rails/Kristi Holl—Who waxed Mad Max?/Gary L.
    Blackwood—Tug, in his own time/Patricia Calvert—New day
    dawning/Joyce Hansen—Family monster/Pamela F. Service—Just
    a theory/H.M. Hoover—The wall/Marion Dane Bauer—A sheepish
    answer/Carol Kendall and Yao-wen Li—An education/Marie G.
    Lee.
        Summary: Includes short stories of various genres, author
    interviews, and an introduction to each genre.
        ISBN 0-8027-8424-0 (hardcover).
        1. Children's stories, American. [1. Short stories.] I. Asher,
    Sandy.
    PZ5.B985   1996
    [Fic]—dc20   95-26355
                                                                         CIP
                                                                          AC

"A Time to Stand Up" copyright © 1996 by Elaine Marie Alphin
"The Wall" copyright © 1996 by Marion Dane Bauer
"Who Waxed Mad Max?" copyright © 1996 by Gary L. Blackwood
"Tug, in His Own Time" copyright © 1996 by Patricia Calvert
"New Day Dawning" copyright © 1996 by Joyce Hansen
"Echoes Down the Rails" copyright © 1996 by Kristi Holl
"Just a Theory" copyright © 1996 by H. M. Hoover
"Flying Away" copyright © 1996 by Angela Johnson
"A Sheepish Answer" copyright © 1996 by Carol Kendall and Yao-wen Li
"An Education" copyright © 1996 by Marie G. Lee
"Alligator Mystique" copyright © 1996 by Barbara Robinson
"Family Monster" copyright © 1996 by Pamela F. Service

Photo on page 66 by Pat Laurie
Photo on page 93 by Austin Hansen
Photo on page 162 by Karl Jacoby

Printed in the United States of America
10 9 8 7 6 5 4 3 2 1

Contents

But That's Another Story

Welcome

THERE WAS a time when I read nothing but animal stories: *Misty of Chincoteague, Lassie Come Home,* and others like them, over and over again. I *loved* those stories! But the day came when I began to wonder, "What else is there?" That's when I discovered all kinds of stories—about dragons and Dracula, pioneers and pirates, families that were just like mine and families that I *wished* were mine.

What else is there?

A lot!

Animal stories are one *genre* of fiction. The word *genre* was borrowed from the French ("ZHAHN-ruh"). It means *kind* or *category.* You can easily recognize other stories of this genre: Their main focus will always be on one or more animals and how they interact with other animals or with people. In this book, Patricia Calvert's "Tug, in His Own Time" is just such a story.

There are many fiction genres. Each has its own rules, its own fictional world, and its own special rewards for readers.

Contemporary realism captures intense moments in the lives of modern characters and lets you see those moments through their eyes. In Angela Johnson's "Flying Away" and Marie G. Lee's "An Education," you'll get to know two young people who are struggling in very different ways to deal with a parent's disturbing decision.

Humor often looks at everyday events in a lighthearted way, and everyday events at the Cafe Florida turn hilarious when David dons a fuzzy green suit in Barbara Robinson's "Alligator Mystique."

When lightning flashes and dark storm clouds roll in, the stage is set for *suspense,* as in "Echoes Down the Rails," by Kristi Holl. And for even more serious shivers, there's the irresistible *horror* that lurks deep within Marion Dane Bauer's "The Wall."

On the other hand, Halloween's more sticky than scary if you choose the right clues and corner the culprit in Gary L. Blackwood's *detective story* "Who Waxed Mad Max?"

Folktales are fanciful yarns handed down from one generation to the next, with all their wit and wisdom intact. You'll discover "A Sheepish Answer" to the problem of jealousy in the ancient Chinese tale retold by Carol Kendall and Yaowen Li. *Historical fiction* also takes you into the past, but back to events that either were or could have been real. Visit a plantation as the Civil War ends in Joyce Hansen's "New Day Dawning."

Science fiction and *time-travel fantasy* explore possibilities across both time and space. Check out the aliens hovering over a softball field in H. M. Hoover's "Just a Theory." Then tour Scotland's Loch Ness—today and long ago—and meet the "Family Monster" created by legend and Pamela F. Service.

Unfamiliar places can mean unexpected danger. In Elaine Marie Alphin's "A Time to Stand Up," Eric visits Zimbabwe, Africa, confronts ruthless poachers, and survives an *adventure story.*

No two stories are alike. That's because no two writers

are alike, as you'll notice when you read the author interviews that follow these stories. Everyone sees the world in a unique way; everyone has unique tales to tell.

Here are twelve of them.

—SANDY ASHER

1. CONTEMPORARY REALISM

THE PEOPLE, places and events in *realistic fiction* seem to come straight out of real life. They may even resemble people, places, and events in our own lives. It's as if we've met the characters before. Or, if we haven't met them yet, we wouldn't be surprised to bump into them one day at school or the supermarket.

Sometimes these characters introduce us to situations we wouldn't ordinarily be able to experience: Through reading, city dwellers can pitch hay on a farm; country cousins can ride a subway train.

When the story's well written, we may feel closer to its characters than to flesh-and-blood people we know. That's because a good writer can take us inside a character's mind and heart and reveal secret dreams and fears that real people seldom share. As we come to understand the characters, we learn about ourselves and other people as well.

But realistic stories are still fiction. Details from the real world—cereal and songs, T-shirts and toothbrushes—combine with a writer's imagination to create a new story world that looks real and sounds real but isn't. This world exists only between the covers of a book; it comes alive only when a reader begins reading.

A realistic story set in modern times is called *contemporary realism*. Angela Johnson's "Flying Away" is an example of contemporary realism. The radio is playing, breakfast is served, and you are right there. . . .

Flying Away

ANGELA JOHNSON

It's our last day in Hopeville. I could tell when Mama got up, looked out the window, and shook her head at the field out back. Brother and Cookie keep eating their Cap'n Crunch and singing to the radio. I wait a few minutes before I start eating. Know the food won't go down anyway.

Mama watches the backyard with one hand on her hip and the other around a big old coffee mug we gave her last Mother's Day. It's shaped like a plane.

Mama loves airplanes.

She always talks about one day just getting on a bus going to the airport and flying away. She says it would sure be something. All of us on the plane like that—flying away.

Mama talks about how she'd ask the stewardess for a pillow and a ginger ale even. She talks about how close we'd all be to the stars up there—flying away.

Another song comes on the radio that Brother and Cookie know. They wave their spoons in the air and snap their fingers. Brother rocks back and forth on his chair and laughs when Cookie starts to do the same.

I watch how they move and walk closer to the radio— trying to feel what they hear, feeling bad that they don't know we're moving.

Brother and Cookie wouldn't know yet. They're thinking about the bus ride to school and what they'll say to their friends when they get there. Cookie's thinking about how she just got settled this summer and met a few people at the carnival last month.

Brother's thinking about football and how he wants to get this car. It's red, and his eyes shine when he talks about it.

I know what they're both thinking. I always have. I can hear their thoughts in my mind, but that's the only place I can hear.

I don't miss hearing sound 'cause I don't remember ever hearing it. They say I did, though. Mama says I heard sound until I was about one—then it went away. She says that the few words I'd spoken went away too. But that's OK.

I feel so bad for Brother and Cookie I clear their bowls off the table before they can put them in the sink themselves. Cookie smiles the same as Brother does. They're twins and do so much alike. I've always wanted to be a twin. I've always wanted somebody to hear me before I tried to hear them. Mama comes close. She turns from the window and looks at me the moment Brother and Cookie leave the kitchen.

She knows I know.

They got everything you'd ever need in the By the Creek Road Truckstop. They got toothbrushes with elephant heads and beef jerky. They got thick pencils with troll heads on the ends of them and T-shirts that glow in the dark. Mama laughs at something the waitress says and bites into a fried bologna sandwich. She says you can only get good ones on the road.

Cookie moves closer to Brother in the corner of the booth and rolls her eyes at Mama. Brother stirs his Coke with a spoon over and over, never looking up. Mama leans over and picks up one of my fries. She eats it and smiles at me. I smile back at her and feel sorry for Cookie and Brother. They still can't understand about leaving. They don't want to understand.

By the time Brother and Cookie got out of school today all our clothes were packed in the van, and Mama had told the landlord and our schools that we weren't coming back. We never do.

On the way out of town she went to the store where she'd worked and walked out with a big smile on her face. Brother and Cookie didn't say anything until we passed the high school. Mama had to pull to the side of the road and I closed my eyes. I didn't want to feel or hear what was in their minds and on their lips, 'cause they would never understand the leaving.

Once Mama packed us up in the middle of the night and had us gone before morning. She'd been talking about planting a garden in the front yard at dinner. Things change just like that with Mama. Always have. I know something, though. I know why we leave a lot. Mama told me about it one night when the air was so still I felt like I couldn't breathe. I could have drank a tank of cool water that night. Mama brought me a Popsicle and turned on the porch light so I could see her hands in the dark of the night.

Mama's hands danced to me that night. She told me about the mountains and oceans she wanted us to see. She told me about places that only a few people had been. She wanted us to see them. She told me it wasn't the place that was so important as the trip getting there. Me, her, Cookie, and Brother were special. Nobody like us in the whole world, she said.

Special.

Cookie's over in the pasture, sitting next to a cow, reading. Brother sits next to her, staring up at the cow. Mama is on top of the car, smoking. She winks at me from underneath her sunglasses. She's out of reach. I can't put her cigarette out like I usually do when she puts it down for a second in an ash tray. I wonder if smoke makes sounds.

I wonder if the big trucks that blow by us makes sounds, too. I wave to Mama to ask her but she doesn't see me or my hand signs. She just looks ahead of us on down the road.

I've been saving things in a big box from all the places we've lived. I got postcards that say HELLO FROM HOPEVILLE, OH the first day we moved there. The woman at the drugstore smiled at me and talked for a long time. She seemed so nice I bought two postcards. Brother thought it was funny, but never did tell me what she was saying. The drugstore smelled like bubble gum and newspaper. Most of them do.

I always keep my box close to me. Never know when you might want to remember. Mama doesn't like to remember. She never talks about where we've been. Cookie and Brother usually just turn the radio up and look out the car windows. The music must be real loud 'cause I can feel it. It shakes me.

Mama just smokes and drives on.

They all leave me to think about mountains and rivers and places only a few people have been. We've lived in places that looked like they were forgotten about a thousand years ago. Hard to believe anybody stayed there at all. I think about mountains and rivers a lot. . . .

I used to think that mountains made noises, but Brother told me they didn't, and I don't know why but it made me sad. We'd gone through the Rockies once and I think it was the first time I missed my hearing. I just knew those mountains should have been making some kind of beautiful sounds. I don't know which kinds, but the sounds should've made everybody smile. All we got was wide-eyed and open-mouthed.

When we were really high up in the mountains, Mama pulled over to the side of the road, got out of the car, and looked up for almost an hour. She pulled me out of the car and put my face close to hers. She mouthed the words, "It's like flying." So I looked up too. It was. . . .

We've been days on the road when we pull up to George, Kansas. I know this is the place. Brother and Cookie know it, too. They sink way down in the backseat. Mama makes a U-turn into a gas station, gets out, and asks the man who comes over to pump our gas something. Brother and Cookie are walking down the street when I look in the backseat again. They've found a Dairy Queen down the way, and Mama is sipping coffee out of a paper cup, laughing with the man.

Hello, George.

If you know where to look, you can get a house full of furniture for under a hundred dollars. It takes some time, though. You just have to know where to look. Mama knows. She always knows. In George, Kansas, it's Suzy's Used. That's all. Used everything at Suzy's. Suzy watches me as I sit on one of her chairs. It's velvet and blue. I smile at Suzy, then she turns to Mama and says something. Mama buys everything she needs for our house next door to the Dairy Queen.

Brother and Cookie saw the for rent sign in the window as they were buying Buster Bars. My room overlooks the Dairy Queen parking lot. I smell chocolate a lot and like the way the sign lights up my room. Anyway . . . we find all that we need at Suzy's. Suzy signs to me to have a good time in my new house.

Cookie's not talking to Mama yet. Brother talks to her. Mama smiles all the time now. We're someplace else and she's happy. . . .

❧

I'll bet you can see a hundred miles from every direction out of George. Brother and Cookie started school yesterday. It's a county school. I guess there aren't enough people in George for one whole school. They don't even wave to me when they get on the bus. I watch from the roof of our house as they find a seat and scrunch up in it together.

I've been spending a lot of time on the roof. Mama brings me juice and sandwiches when she thinks about it. She says I'll be going to school in a few days. I met my teacher yesterday. She smells like oranges and her eyes twinkle. I like the way her hands look when she signs to me. They're nice hands. Mama even seems to like her.

Mama's been busy getting the house ready. After one day in a new house, Mama makes it look like we've lived there forever. She says she can't waste any time getting us settled. Home is important—even if we have more than three a year. We never have lived in an apartment. Mama doesn't believe in them. She always says, "You gotta have a yard."

The first thing we do in our new homes is to have dinner in the front yard. Once we ate chili in Minnesota in the middle of January on our porch. Brother and Cookie coughed for two weeks. Mama fed them cough medicine and laughed about getting used to the cold. Cookie says Mama is crazy, even if she does find us good homes.

I hear Mama in the house hammering a nail in the wall. She's hanging up the velvet picture of dogs playing pool. She loves that one. We've had about ten of them. Mama always tries to find the picture wherever we move. There's a lot of velvet dog paintings in the Midwest.

Mama is beside me now. She got up here by climbing out of Cookie's bedroom window, just like I did. She lies back and looks straight up into the sky. I can hear everything she thinks. Everything.

Brother and Cookie don't want to find new mountains and rivers anymore. They're getting on a bus this morning, but not the school bus. I lean against Mama in the cold while Cookie and Brother stand ahead of us and keep stepping off the curb in front of Suzy's Used, to be the first to see the Greyhound bus. It will take them away from us and George, Kansas.

Cookie and Brother hug and kiss me when the bus pulls up. They put their suitcases and duffel bags into the side and blow on their hands to warm them. They both turn to Mama. When she nods to them, they get on the bus to Aunt May's in California. I run behind the bus as long as I can. Mama walks away in the opposite direction.

When I get home Mama is drinking coffee up on the roof. I watch her looking all over George. She looks in the direction of the bus that just took Cookie and Brother away. She sees me and waves me up. There's a little time before my school bus gets here. Mama pulls me across the roof tiles to her and talks to me.

Mostly about nothing. Her hands are stiff from the cold—even with the hot coffee. Some of her signing I can't understand, so I close my eyes and lie on my back. Being up here is almost as good as flying. You can see everything and the sky is clear. You can look right over George into forever, and maybe even see the next place you might have to leave for.

When I turn to Mama there are tears running down her face, but all I can think is that she should be happy. She's taught Cookie and Brother how to fly.

Meet the Author

Angela Johnson was born in Tuskegee, Alabama, and attended Kent State University in Ohio, where she now lives. Stories told to her by her grandfather and father and read to her in school inspired her to become a writer. "Book people came to life," she says. "They sat beside me in Maple Grove School. That is when I knew. I asked for a diary . . . and have not stopped writing."

As a teenager, she wrote "personal and angry" punk poetry she didn't want to publish, but now "I hope my writing is universal and speaks to everyone who reads it." *Toning the Sweep,* her first novel, won the Coretta Scott King Award.

BOOKS BY ANGELA JOHNSON

NOVELS
Humming Whispers
Toning the Sweep

BOARD BOOKS
Joshua by the Sea
Joshua's Night Whispers
Mama Bird, Baby Birds
Rain Feet

PICTURE BOOKS
Do Like Kyla
The Girl Who Wore Snakes
Julius
The Leaving Morning
One of Three
Shoes Like Miss Alice
Tell Me a Story, Mama
When I Am Old with You

More About "Flying Away"

SANDY ASHER: Where did you get the idea for this story?

ANGELA JOHNSON: "Flying Away" was written at a time when one of my friends was dealing with so many problems, she thought the only way she could leave her problems behind was to run away. It made me wonder how older runaways (the narrator's mother) may have started their habits.

SA: So we see Cookie and Brother starting the same habit.

AJ: Yes, the siblings of the narrator learn from their mother that you can always leave any trouble behind. Dealing with troubles doesn't seem to be an option for them. The older children continue the habits of their mother, while the youngest is more introspective about it all.

SA: True, he thinks about the situation but doesn't try to change it or get out of it. What made you choose a deaf narrator?

AJ: I wanted the story to be his so much that the reader is almost cut off from what everyone else in the story is doing. He sees the beauty of leaving it all behind—and the pitfalls. I believe that he can be introspective because, one, he is a bit removed from his family through his deafness and two, he is so young and has no real control over his mother's actions.

I believe that a good story can be told by someone who makes no judgment on the proceedings. When a narrator starts judging the story, it tends to trail off in a different direction. In "Flying Away," I want to give readers a feeling of perpetual mobility. I want them to feel that any minute the mother may move again and the children will continue to circle her like satellites. I want them to feel the newness of every situation as it happens.

SA: This story is contemporary realism, but it's a part of reality, as Mama says, where "only a few people have been." How do you convince readers that "special" characters like Mama are real, even though most of us have never met anyone quite like her?

AJ: There are certain emotions that are universal. I find that people are the same. Some are quirky, but they have the same emotions. I tend to make most of the characters in my stories live a bit on the strange and wonderful side. I find if you leave the creative door open and let these people in, it becomes easy to write about them.

Someone once told me that he only read stories that mirrored his own life, and I thought, how boring! Isn't it important to go someplace else when you read? Realism is so personal, but it doesn't have to be boring. I talk about the family stopping to view the mountains and the idea that the narrator thinks that the mountains make noise. If you have never seen color, what would be your reality of red? I try to imagine that. My stories don't mirror my life at all.

SA: Readers who have enjoyed "Flying Away" will want to take a look at your novels, *Toning the Sweep* and *Humming Whispers*. What other authors of contemporary realism would you recommend to them?

AJ: I would recommend anything by Virginia Hamilton and Avi. They do wonderfully intimate portraits of individuals. One of the first young adult novels I read as an adult was Virginia Hamilton's *Sweet Whispers Brother Rush*. I cried through much of the book. I remember thinking, "What is this book doing to me?" I had never been so moved by words in my whole life. I thought that it was magic.

Years later, when I began writing myself, I realized what the author had done. She touched primal emotions—love, loss, pain, pleasure—but she didn't tell you how you were supposed to feel. I wanted to evoke emotions that moved readers to tears, happiness, anger, and recognition. I never know if I am doing this when I'm writing, though. I don't really think about how others will feel when I'm writing. It's so personal when it's happening. I go with my emotions, and hope that they work for those who read my stories.

2. HUMOR

STORY CHARACTERS often find themselves caught in unfamiliar situations. Sometimes the results are serious, as in "Flying Away." And sometimes they're very funny, as in the next story, "Alligator Mystique" by Barbara Robinson.

"Whenever you take a character out of his normal surroundings and plunk him down somewhere else," she says, "you have the makings of a funny situation."

That's especially true when the character belongs to a writer who tends to see humor in all kinds of situations. Barbara Robinson is that kind of writer. "This story, like many of my stories, contains a mental picture that is (or seems to me) funny. The trick is to put that picture into words, for the reader to see. I hope readers of this story can see David in his fuzzy green suit, sitting by the palm tree!"

Humor may spring from a wacky situation, a wry character, or witty narration and dialogue. You'll find all of that and more in this story. "Alligator Mystique" is *contemporary* and it's *realistic*. But more than anything else, it's *funny*. That makes it an example of the genre called *humorous fiction*.

Alligator Mystique
~~ BARBARA ROBINSON

My sister Marsha's boyfriend is the alligator at this restaurant called Cafe Florida. According to Marsha, nobody knows this except our family, which is my mother and father and Marsha and me . . . and Bruce boyfriend's family, the Stapletons.

"That's crazy," I told her. "What about the other people who work at the restaurant?"

"Only the manager knows," she said. "No one else knows, so they can preserve the mystique. You probably don't understand about that, David."

She's right. I don't understand alligator mystique—big green thing comes walking in every night at six o'clock and nobody says, "Who's in there?" Huh-uh.

Of course I'm never there at six o'clock or, in fact, any other time, although it *is* safe to feed me in grown-up restaurants. "Pretty nice manners," my mother always says, "for a boy not quite twelve years old."

I figure, when she says "*pretty* nice" she is giving me some room in case I accidentally drop a bowl of soup on the floor or get stuck with a mouthful of something I don't recognize in time—like, once, a snail, all wrapped up in some kind of juicy bread. Marsha went and hid in the bathroom that time, but I don't know what else I was supposed to do with the snail—it wouldn't go *down*.

Anyway, when I'm part of the family dinner out, dinner

out is burgers and fries at Mickey D's—lots of burgers and lots of fries. This is fine with me. It's also fine with Marsha, because she says Bruce can't do his best job if the restaurant is full of friends and family. "Even his own parents don't go to Café Florida," she says. "They don't want to make him nervous."

My father says that if he were Mr. Stapleton, he would be the nervous one, waiting all the time for somebody to slap him on the back and say, "So! You're the alligator's father!"

"Why doesn't Bruce get a normal job," he says, "bagging at the supermarket or pumping gas?"

Big sniff from Marsha. "He *has* a normal job."

I let, maybe, half a second go by. "Only if he plans to live in a swamp."

Then, while my mother is saying, "Now, now, David," and "Now, now, Marsha," and my father is saying, ". . . or lawn care. Good part-time jobs in lawn care," Marsha lands on me.

"What could you possibly know about it?" she says. "You've never had any kind of job and probably never will because all you know how to do is eat!" And she stomps off.

"Hey!" I yell after her. "I'm just a kid, remember? Who's going to give me a job?"

Who? . . . Bruce, that's who, two days later.

"It's . . . uh . . . pretty easy," he said, "and . . . uh . . ."

Marsha took over. "It's *very* easy," she said. "You just walk around and greet people, especially children. In between times you sit in the lobby beside the palm tree. You sort of . . . lounge . . . beside the palm tree. It's only four hours, six till ten tonight, and Mom and Dad are going out so they don't even have to know."

She was moving right along as if this was a normal everyday thing, like calling up a replacement from the bench at a hockey game—"You, David, go in for the alligator!"

"Wait a minute," I said. "I can't do this!"

"You have to," Marsha said, and she explained again that they suddenly had these free tickets to this concert by Apples and Sweet Gotcha. ". . . but Bruce can't call out from work now, not on Saturday night, and still keep his job."

"And . . . uh . . ." Here came Bruce, with something to say. "You . . . uh . . . fit the suit."

I *am* big for my age (lots of burgers, lots of fries) and Bruce is sort of short and skinny, so that part was all right.

"See?" Marsha said, zipping me up the back. "It's just a little bit big, but that won't matter. Walk around, David, see how it feels."

It felt okay—like fuzzy green pajamas with feet and arms and . . .

"Look out!" Marsha yelled, as the tail whipped up and around. "You turned too fast," she said. "You have to turn slowly or your tail will fly up in the air."

And then, while I was trying to get hold of the zipper and get out (because what if I forget to turn slowly and my tail wipes out some waitress with six dinners on a tray?), Marsha slapped the alligator head on me.

"It's perfect, David," she said. "Look at yourself."

"Where?" I said. "How?" First I can't turn around, now I can't see . . . or talk, because from inside the alligator head I sounded like some old person at the bottom of a well.

"You're not . . . uh . . . supposed to talk." Bruce moved the head up and down and around till I could see out of the little alligator eyeholes. "Because . . . uh . . . what would an alligator . . . uh . . . say?"

Not much, I thought, if Bruce was the alligator.

But then, money changed hands—twenty-five dollars, from Bruce to me—so, at six o'clock that night, I flap-slapped into Cafe Florida.

"The gator's here," somebody called back toward the manager's office, and one of the waitresses poked me in the ribs and giggled. "I don't care who you are," she said, "I think you're cute," and off she went, to wait on tables. So Marsha was right—mystique.

I stood around, wishing someone would tell me what to do, but of course I was supposed to *know* what to do. "Walk around, greet people . . ." Sounds easy till it's time to do it.

So I sat down by the palm tree, which also sounds easy till it's time to do it as an alligator. What do you do with your big green hands? and your big green feet? I crossed one leg over the other one, leaned on one arm, began to sweat . . .

"Oh, there's the alligator. Look, Ethel, there's the alligator!" These ladies came over, patted me on the head, shook my loose hand.

Then came a family with little kids. "Go say hello to the alligator," the mother told them. "You wanted to come here 'specially to see him."

Sometimes I was a surprise—"Oh, look what they have at this restaurant!" but usually not—"Do you remember me?" one little girl said, "from last time?"

I saw some kids from my school, but I knew they'd stay away. No sixth grade kid is going to hang around with the hired alligator . . . except Hot Dog Brian Kelso, who walked up, looked me in the eye (actually, sort of looked me in the forehead) and said, very tough, "Get a life."

By now I was pretty good at this lounging-by-the-palm-tree part, but it didn't last. The manager came up, smiled around at the customers, and whispered in my ear, "Come on, Bruce, I don't pay you to sit here all night. Get up and circulate. Start in the back room."

The back room is where they put big parties with kids, so I was back there for a long time, shaking hands and letting mothers and fathers talk to me about what their kids were eating or not eating—"I'll bet the alligator likes green beans" or "Let's ask the alligator to choose your dessert." I would nod my head up and down about the green beans or the broccoli, and point to the fudge brownie on the dessert cart, and let kids feel my fuzzy suit . . . and by the time I moved into the middle dining room I was feeling pretty good. Waitresses thought I was cute, little kids thought I was a big, green, fuzzy friend, nobody knew who I really was, and I was earning twenty-five dollars.

Then I saw my parents.

They were sitting at a table against the wall, and I turned to go the other way and . . .

"Watch it!" somebody yelled . . . too late.

It was, of course, *their* waitress, and *their* tray of food— salad and rolls all over the floor.

Somebody cleaned it up and the waitress came back with new food and apologized to my parents for the delay. "We just have to watch out for our alligator!" she said.

"Oh!" My mother sat up in her seat and leaned across the table. "We certainly don't want to blame the alligator. We just *love* the alligator." She looked straight at me. "We think you're very good at this job."

Then, as the waitress moved away, she grabbed one of my green paws. "Oh, Bruce, I'm so sorry! Marsha always said we shouldn't come here and make you nervous, and that's exactly what we did. You won't get fired, will you? Should we speak to the manager? I just wish . . ."

My father said, "Helen, people are looking at you. You're talking to this alligator as if he's your own flesh and blood."

"Well, I'm very fond of Bruce. I'm very fond of you, Bruce."

I could see us in the mirror wall—my mother looking worried, my father looking embarrassed, and me looking like your average everyday restaurant alligator.

Suddenly this whole thing felt like a bad Halloween trick, and I thought, This is as sneaky as it gets. This is worse than listening outside the girls' bathroom or reading Marsha's diary. What if they say something private to Bruce, thinking I'm Bruce? What if they say something private about me, not knowing I'm me?

"To tell the truth," my father said, "this was my idea, to get a look at you on the job. After all, Bruce, Marsha is . . ."

I couldn't stand it. "I'm not Bruce," I said. I'd forgotten about my voice inside the alligator head, and it even scared me.

It scared my mother. She sort of squealed and jumped and dropped my paw, and my father said, "What? What was that?" I heard a lady at the next table ask her friend, "Did that alligator say something?" and a little boy who was passing by stopped and just stood there, staring at me.

I didn't know what to do, or what to say, or whether to say anything. Should I explain? Lie? Tell the truth? Get out of there?

"Hey . . . Hey . . ." It was the little boy, pulling on my suit, and I remembered him now, from the other room. He was the green beans. "Will you take me to the bathroom, alligator?"

Normally . . . I don't think so. But right then, I grabbed his hand and took off.

When my parents left the restaurant I was back at the palm tree, hoping they would just go out the door. But here they came, straight for me, so I had to make up my mind—tell them? or not tell them?

"You probably wonder what that was all about," my mother said. "You see, we thought you were my daughter's boyfriend," and my father said, "He's the regular alligator."

That did it. Because of course Bruce wouldn't *be* the regular alligator anymore if I told them who I was—maybe took off my head to prove it—right here in the lobby of Cafe Florida, for everyone to see and hear.

So I didn't tell them. And I still haven't told them. And I don't think I'll ever tell them. . . .

Man, *that's* mystique!

Meet the Author

Barbara Robinson was born in a small town called Portsmouth, Ohio. "I always seem to place my characters in small towns, too," she says, "though I've lived since in big-city suburbs— Pittsburgh, Boston, and now Philadelphia. I went to Allegheny College, in Pennsylvania, where I studied theater—great preparation for writing books!

"Like most writers, I'd rather read than eat; my favorite place to be is on the beach at Cape Cod; and my secret ambition (not so secret, really) is to be a dancer . . . provided I could still write stories!"

Barbara Robinson has two daughters, Carolyn and Margie. Along with her books and short stories, she wrote the play and film versions of *The Best Christmas Pageant Ever*.

BOOKS BY BARBARA ROBINSON

NOVELS
The Best Christmas Pageant Ever
My Brother Louis Measures Worms
Temporary Times, Temporary Places
The Worst Best School Year Ever

PICTURE BOOK
The Fattest Bear in the First Grade

More about "Alligator Mystique"

BARBARA ROBINSON: This story grew out of a visit to a restaurant where there was, in fact, somebody dressed up in
an alligator suit. I really wanted to know who was in
there, how he or she liked the job, whether the suit was
hot or itchy . . . things like that. My family wouldn't let
me talk to the alligator (too embarrassing, they said), so
I had to write the story to get some answers.

SANDY ASHER: Because of its lighthearted, often casual style,
humor seems easier to write than other kinds of fiction,
but many writers find it more difficult to do well. Why
is that, do you think?

BR: Mostly because we can't assume anything about the
reader's response. If we've written a scary story, or a sad
story, or a suspenseful story, there are certain reactions
we can count on . . . but humor is entirely individual and
unpredictable.

SA: I have no trouble predicting humor when I pick up one
of your stories! What books—your own and favorites by
other authors—would you recommend to readers who
enjoyed your story and want to read more humorous fiction?

BR: Of my own, I'd particularly suggest *The Best Christmas
Pageant Ever*. The characters are put into a completely

unnatural situation, for them—a little more involved than an alligator suit, but it's the same idea. In *The Worst Best School Year Ever*, the situations are unexpected, and in *My Brother Louis Measures Worms*, most of the stories involve misunderstandings and mistaken identities—of people and worms.

Then I'd suggest *The Carp in the Bathtub* by Barbara Cohen, *Be a Perfect Person in Just Three Days* by Stephen Manes, the Wayside School books by Louis Sachar, and Jerry Spinelli's books, especially *Space Station Seventh Grade*.

3. ADVENTURE

U NFAMILIAR SITUATIONS can be funny, but they can also be dangerous. Lost and alone in strange surroundings, faced with life-threatening obstacles, characters in *adventure stories* use their wit and every ounce of their strength to battle their way back to safety.

Adventure stories often take place in exotic locations and pit their characters against forces of nature—raging rivers, unexplored wilderness, daunting mountain peaks. Human enemies may also threaten the main characters, but the greatest challenge comes from within. As a character digs deep for the courage and stamina to survive, he or she must face and overcome lifelong weaknesses and fears.

In "A Time to Stand Up" by Elaine Marie Alphin, Eric Foster finds himself on a game ranch in Zimbabwe, Africa. He'd rather be back home practicing football, but a new acquaintance leads him deep into the bush, where their lives—and far more—are soon at stake.

A Time to Stand Up
✎ ELAINE MARIE ALPHIN

"Make up your mind, Eric," Hal Foster said impatiently. "Are you coming to see the calf or not?"

"Not," Eric said, ducking his head furiously and kicking at the black dirt of Africa. When his father had suggested the visit to a game ranch in Zimbabwe, Eric had imagined a chance for them to get to know each other again after the long divorce proceedings. His father seemed like a stranger—he hadn't even asked about Eric's play as linebacker on the state football championship team last season.

The open spaces of Africa had sounded like a solution, but ever since they'd arrived his father had been talking into his microcassette recorder with the ranch owner, Ross Wilson. Eric had been dragged from one end of the hundred-thousand-acre ranch to the other. He'd listened to discussions on breeding, radio tracking, cattle encroachment, population balance, poaching, until he was sick of it. Why had his father bothered to drag him along? Eric thought of summer football practice. He'd probably lose his starting position because he was missing it, and his father didn't care.

That morning they had driven the Land Rovers down rugged dirt roads, lurching through the changing landscape to the southeastern sector of the ranch to inspect a windmill-driven water pump. Then they'd gone north to check out a black rhino mud wallow.

Eric had admired the rhinoceros. Independent and truculent, it had stood its ground, ready to charge. But when they remained motionless, the wind carrying their scent away, its tiny eyes had squinted nearsightedly, its ears pivoting like radar seeking them.

"That one's safe," Ross told Eric's father. "I wish I could get them all in one place, but they're so territorial."

Then they'd driven to a clearing bounded by flat-topped acacia trees and eaten lunch under a vast blue sky. Eric had worked up the nerve to ask his father to go back to the lodge with him, when Ross suggested heading northeast to check on a rhino and calf. That was it.

"I'll go back to the lodge," he told his father curtly.

Ross exchanged an impatient look with Hal Foster. "You can go back in one of the Rovers with Nicodemus," the rancher said.

Eric grabbed his knapsack and turned sharply. He knew he wasn't being polite, but the Ndebele gamekeeper driving him back to the lodge wasn't what he wanted. He wanted his father—fat chance. The gamekeepers giggled as he tramped back toward the vehicles, holding their hands up to cover their mouths. He didn't know why the sight of him was so hilarious.

One youngster wasn't laughing. He stood apart, leaning on a stick. He wore torn denim shorts and a dirty T-shirt like the others, but his face had a sad expression—a lonely look that probably mirrored Eric's own. Their eyes met, and the kid stood straighter. He pointed hesitantly toward a thorn thicket covered with new blossoms.

Eric glanced at the others, but they had clustered around Ross's Land Rover. "Can you take me to the lodge?" he asked. "Ross said to ride with Nicodemus, but I'm sick of being a laughingstock. We're not far, are we? We could walk."

The kid jabbed his stick at the ground, and Eric saw it had a handmade point bound onto it—a kid's spear. He almost grinned but then remembered how it felt to be laughed at. And he didn't want to hurt this kid's feelings—he was the first person who'd been friendly. "My name's Eric."

"Pupho," the kid said in a soft, musical voice. "Come. I take you."

Eric looked back, but his father was talking into his recorder. He shouldered his knapsack and defiantly followed Pupho along a twisting game trail into the bush. After about ten minutes they broke into open grassland, and he squinted at the sun from under the brim of his hat. He felt like Indiana Jones wearing it, but he hadn't believed how hot the African sun could be until he burned the top of his head, right through his hair, that first afternoon. Now he wore it always.

"Hey, Pupho," he said. "You sure we're going the right way?"

Pupho pointed straight ahead. "Shortcut."

That made sense. They'd swung around in the Land Rovers. It was probably much shorter by foot. Eric settled into an easy stride. Every fifteen or twenty minutes they passed another rocky outcropping (Ross had called them kopjies). Eric could hear the rasping of the grass in the breeze and the crisp rustling as an occasional scattering of antelope bounded past, veering away as they caught his scent. He jumped once at a sliding whistle sound.

"Reedbuck," Pupho said, and smiled.

Eric smiled back—the kid wasn't laughing at him.

After another half hour they entered a wooded area wilder than any park Eric had ever hiked through in America. A tiny antelope, a duiker no larger than a dog, came nearly to Eric's boots before bolting. Then a black-and-white bird swooped down, squawking harshly through a curved yellow beak.

Before he could say anything, Eric heard a sound like a popcorn popper gone crazy.

Pupho motioned down.

Eric dropped, pressing himself as deep into the earth as he could. The popping was nearly drowned out by squeals and crashing sounds, then the racket stopped and he heard voices he couldn't understand. There was a strange thudding—the sound was vaguely familiar, but he couldn't place it. Finally the thudding ceased, and the voices gradually dwindled away. He lay there thinking Pupho would say when it was safe to get up.

Eric wasn't sure how long it was before he realized he was alone. He lifted his face and saw the little duiker had returned. Feeling foolish, Eric got to unsteady feet and looked around the deserted woods.

"Pupho?" The name was a croak.

He began to walk in the direction the sounds had come from, slowly at first, then faster once he found a trail. By the changing light he guessed there was a clearing ahead.

He heard new sounds—a tittering, whooping noise like the men's laughter, and also a heavy, flapping noise. Go back, he thought. You don't have to look. But he made himself follow the last twist into the clearing.

A hyena, dyed red to the neck, raised its muzzle and shrieked laughter. Other hyenas hooted and danced back and forth, trying to frighten Eric away. A vulture lifted off a branch and flapped lazily around the clearing before landing nearer to the carcass. Eric ducked back into the trees and pressed his clammy face against rough bark, struggling to control his stomach. He knew now what that thudding had been—an ax, like his father had used cutting firewood when he'd lived at home. And that huge shape in the clearing— nothing but food for vultures and hyenas now—it had been a rhinoceros, like the one he'd admired earlier. The ax blows had hacked off its horns and cut open its body for the scavengers.

Poachers.

He had to get back and radio Ross and his father. But where was the lodge? A weight of betrayal dragged at his shoulders worse than the straps of his knapsack. Pupho had left him, and his father had no idea he was lost. He tried to swallow, but felt only a dry click in his throat. How could the kid just walk out on him?

Eric pulled off his pack and found the canteen. He savored the lukewarm swallow of water on his parched throat—he had never tasted anything as delicious. He tipped the canteen again, then stopped. It was barely half full, and he'd need water later. What he needed now was energy. He found a half-melted chocolate bar and bit off a huge chunk.

The sugar rush sang in his blood, and he told himself that he could find the lodge. It couldn't be that far—a hundred thousand acres sounded huge, but it was only about 150 square miles. The ranch was only sixteen miles across at its widest point. He could do this.

He wanted another swallow of water, but didn't dare. Chewing gum was supposed to make saliva flow—it was worth a try. He found a stick in the bottom of his knapsack, popped it in, and set off toward what he hoped was west.

It didn't take long to clear the woody patch. As he'd hoped, the sun was ahead and on his right. But how far had they come before running into the poachers? And had Pupho been leading him to the lodge at all?

Eric strode on, recalling the ranch layout. If he headed west he'd run into the barbed wire boundary fence in ten miles, max. There was a game reserve in that direction—no people, but he could follow the fence south six or seven miles until he found the main ranch driveway. Anyway, they'd miss him by then. Ross would send the gamekeepers to look for him.

Yeah, he could just see them driving up, laughing at his getting lost. They'd probably planned this trick with Pupho. Well, he wouldn't give them the satisfaction. The black earth soaked up the sun's heat and reflected it back at him, but Eric refused to give up. He drilled at football practice three hours every afternoon and ran laps after that. It's an easy hike, he told himself, no more than a practice. He'd find the lodge on his own, then he'd warn Ross and be a hero, not the butt of a joke. His father would have to notice him then.

He remembered Pupho's friendly smile, and his stomach clenched. Even if it was a joke, once they'd stumbled onto poachers he should have stuck by him. Or maybe he was scared, Eric thought, wiping his forehead under his hat. He remembered what Ross had said about poaching. There had been about 12,000 black rhino in Zambia, just north of Zimbabwe, twenty years ago. Now there wasn't a single one left. They had been killed by poachers, who sold the horns. Some people in Asia ground the horns for potions; others in the

Middle East bought them to make hilts on ceremonial daggers. There were still a few hundred black rhino in Zimbabwe, and game ranchers and wardens were trying to protect them. But poachers were desperate—a single rhino horn sold for more money than they could make in five years of honest work. They planned their raids like military expeditions, and didn't care who they hurt.

Eric's boots skidded on the round pebbles that lined the game trail. Without warning, a cloud of tiny insects clustered around his mouth and nose and the corners of his eyes, like gnats but worse. He fumbled in his pack for repellent and kept going. Ross had told them about mopani bees—they were after his moisture. If he pushed on he'd get out of their territory.

The sugar rush had faded and his boots weighed a ton. When the bees were gone, Eric stopped in the shade of a teak tree and rewarded himself with water. He rolled it around in his mouth before swallowing, but instantly wanted another sip. It was harder to put the canteen away this time, but it felt ominously light. He couldn't risk being without water.

He walked on. There was a thick stand of wild ebony ahead and groves of acacia trees and kopjies dotting the undulating grassland to his right. He set off toward the ebony, chewing steadily and trying to ignore the sun's glare.

Eric almost passed the ebony before he realized the sounds of the African afternoon had changed. He could still hear the grass rustling, and the snorts and grunts of the animals, but he also heard a soft sound he couldn't identify at first—voices! A singsong of voices like the hum at the lodge in the evenings. People.

Eric was about to shout when he realized he didn't know who they were. Ross and his father had gone northeast.

Could they have circled back? But where were the Land Rovers? Suddenly he swallowed his gum, realizing the poachers could still be around. He strained to listen, then sensed someone beside him. Turning wildly, Eric opened his mouth to yell, then recognized Pupho and let his breath out slowly.

"No sound," Pupho breathed, and led the way.

Eric followed him hesitantly, not sure he trusted the kid. Could he be one of the poaching gang?

Pupho motioned low, and Eric squatted and inched forward until he saw a small clearing in the thicket of interwoven branches. Four men sat there, passing a jar of beer and talking. Eric couldn't understand them, but he saw the automatic rifles propped beside them, and an ax. He also saw two drawstring bags made of woven bark strands, a thick black horn bulging the nearest bag.

Eric backed out with Pupho, praying the men's conversation would cover their moves.

In the open, Eric whirled on the other kid. "Tell me what's going on!" he whispered hoarsely.

Pupho pointed toward some acacia trees and set off quickly.

"Okay, now talk," Eric insisted when they reached the trees. "Are you with them?"

Pupho stabbed the turf with his spear. "No! They M'Shona poachers! My family Ndebele gamekeeper for Nkosi Ross."

Eric was torn between relief and anger. "Then why did you leave me after they killed the rhino?"

The kid looked away. "I follow poachers." He looked at Eric. "You bring Nicodemus and Nkosi Ross. Nkosi Ross kill poachers."

Eric frowned. "Why don't you warn Ross?"

"No one hear me," Pupho said. "Sometimes cousin sees me—but then he looks away. You talk to me."

Pupho's the class goat, Eric realized. He dragged out his canteen, and gulped the last swallows. Why bother to save water? Two outcasts lost in open ranchland with a group of poachers—they were goners.

"Last time, I am afraid. See M'Shona cross fence and go to rhino, like today. But shaking heart make me hide. Then rhino dead and no one find M'Shona. I tell what I saw, but too late. Now father suffers shame of coward son. He not see me."

Mine doesn't see me either, thought Eric, but he said nothing. He was turning these poachers in to prove himself, not for some kid who ran out on him.

"I need help," Pupho said, his voice low and desperate. "I need friend."

"Pretty one-sided friendship," Eric shouted, jumping up. "Where were you when I needed help?" He didn't need this kid, he didn't need his father—he didn't need anyone. He strode through the tall elephant grass into the sun, hoping the lodge was that way.

Then Eric heard Pupho's feet slapping behind him and felt a hand grip his shoulder. "They follow us!"

Eric remembered his own voice rising. How could he be so stupid?

"Hide," Pupho said urgently. "Ahead—there—thorn—"

The two boys started for it, then Eric stopped. Pupho was branded a coward because he had hidden, but was Eric any better? He'd always ducked his head and hidden his feelings. Could he hide now?

"You're right," he said. "I'll get Ross."

"Too late!" Pupho cried. "Poachers coming!"

But Eric was already running. Pupho could follow him

or hide again; he didn't care. He shed his pack to run faster, measuring his progress in acacia groves and kopjies as he passed them. He was grateful he'd drunk the water. It flowed through him bringing new strength, and he lengthened his stride. He could almost hear Coach shouting at him, asking what he thought he was saving his legs for. He shut out the burn in his side and thighs, and ran faster. A sixth kopjie— one more grove, then a rise beyond. He aimed for it. He heard the sound of popping again, louder than in the woods. How far behind were the poachers?

A spray of bullets shattered a thorn bush not two yards to his right, but he kept on. I'm running into the sun, he thought—they're shooting into a ball of fire—it's got to blind them. The popping erupted again. I'm not going to make it—how much farther can I run? Stupid to try . . . should have hidden. . . .

Feet pounded beside him, and he saw Pupho's wiry figure. Eric grinned and felt excitement flare inside. Maybe they had a chance.

The boy pointed with his spear, gasping, "Lodge—past hill—you tell—I stop them."

Eric nodded, though he didn't understand. What did Pupho mean he would stop them? Then he topped the rise, chest heaving, and pounded down the slope. Hope swept through him at the sight of thatched roofs below. Suddenly he heard Pupho behind him, his voice high and terrible.

"M'Shona dirty ones! Murderers of innocents! I lay my curse on you!"

Eric turned. Above him on the ridge, silhouetted against the sky, Pupho stood with his arms upraised, his spear clasped in one fist, and Eric realized what Pupho had meant. He had seen Eric was nearly spent, and bought him time with a challenge to the poachers that came straight from a warrior, not a boy.

"Your sons will know your shame! Your bones will be spread for wild dogs!"

Eric tore his eyes away and raced downhill, yelling. The doors of the lodge and other camp buildings opened and men poured into the yard. He saw Ross gesture, and Nicodemus and the others ran to the arms locker.

"Poachers!" Eric shouted. "A rhino!"

He heard Ross shout to Nicodemus, "Hurry! We need proof—the horns!"

How fast could the men climb the ridge? Without evidence, Eric realized his warning would be worthless. His legs rubbery, he forced himself up the slope as the popping erupted briefly. Eric staggered over the ridge and saw two of the poachers dragging another who struggled weakly. And there—one of the poachers was edging into the shadows of the thorn. Clutched to his chest were the bark bags. Eric heard Ross's men thundering up the slope, but in another minute the horns would be gone.

He thought of the proud rhino cut down by these men, and forced his legs to run as though they had rested all day. It's fourth quarter and this is the last play, he told himself grimly. He launched himself at the man in a bone-crunching tackle that hurled them both to the ground. The man tried to twist away, his face desperate, but Eric wrenched the bags free for the most important fumble he'd ever recovered. Then Ross topped the ridge and shouted. The poacher's expression turned to hatred as his body sagged.

Drained, Eric stood, gripping the two woven bark bags. His father and Ross reached him, and he handed the bags to

Ross, surprised when his father's arms wrapped around him fiercely.

"How—" Hal Foster started.

"Pupho," Eric said, straightening. Now he had the time to turn and see the crumpled, motionless form on the ridge.

The men looked at each other. "One of the gamekeepers' boys," Ross said slowly. "His family calls him Pupho. It means 'Dreamer.' He failed to report poachers last year, and they took a rhino then, too. The gamekeepers act like he's dead—no one talks to him."

Hal Foster spoke rapidly into his recorder.

He just needed a friend, Eric thought, an ache growing in his chest. "He reported it this time," he told the men. "He bought me the time to get help." He blinked, staring at the ridge where Pupho's curse had frightened the poachers into brief immobility.

Nicodemus stood there, holding Pupho's unconscious body. "Do not sorrow, Nkosana Eric. Pupho now Ndebele warrior. All people see Pupho, always."

The gamekeeper turned away to carry Pupho down to the camp. Eric started after him, then stopped. Nicodemus could help the boy best now. Pupho had made his decision to stand up for himself, and for his friend, despite the consequences. It was time Eric stood up for himself.

"Dad," he began, "I need to talk to you—about Pupho, and about me."

His father turned, holding the recorder to him.

"Not to that thing," Eric said, "to you—to figure out how you and I can be a family again."

His father stared at the recorder, then switched it off. Eric could almost feel Pupho's hand on his shoulder as the blood-red sun dropped toward the distant horizon.

Meet the Author

Elaine Marie Alphin graduated from Rice University in Houston, Texas, with majors in history, English, and political science. She also studied medieval military history in England and Italy. Her professional writing career began at *Houston City Magazine,* where she worked as a feature writer. Since then, she's published numerous articles and stories in many national magazines, including *Highlights for Children, Cricket,* and *Disney Adventures.* Her first novel, *The Ghost Cadet,* was a Best Book nominee in fourteen states and won the Virginia Young Readers Award.

❧

BOOKS BY ELAINE MARIE ALPHIN

NOVELS
The Ghost Cadet
The Proving Ground
Tournament of Time

CHAPTER BOOK
A Bear for Miguel

NONFICTION
The Vacuum Cleaner Venture

More About "A Time to Stand Up"

ELAINE MARIE ALPHIN: I spent a month in Africa exploring game parks and game ranches. Poaching (illegal taking of game, as opposed to licensed sport hunting) is the single greatest threat to wildlife, far surpassing habitat encroachment by human settlements. Because of the tremendous profits to be made from illegal sales of rhino horns, elephant tusks, and other animal parts, poachers are willing to take great risks, confronting game wardens and pulling off killing raids on solitary animals like the rhinoceros, and even on herds of elephants, with military precision.

SANDY ASHER: Do adventure story writers have to experience the locale and the adventure in person?

EMA: Seeing a place and even living there for a while enables the writer to describe it naturally in a story. Especially with an exotic locale like Zimbabwe, it was important to use my own sense of discovery and wonder to make Eric's first impression of the bush believable.

But that's not the same as the writer facing an identical danger as the character in his or her story. The details of Eric's fear and courage and determination have to be authentic, but not necessarily because I have confronted poachers. Instead, I use my memories of facing down my own demons, and transform those emotions into Eric's feelings. The passion comes from the writer's life and experiences, but the plot of the story comes from the writer's imagination.

SA: An adventure story isn't just about physical survival, is it?

EMA: When a character is facing a life-and-death situation, he must face himself before he faces his enemy. Physical survival is essential, but the main conflict is really psychological. It is Eric's need to prove himself to his father that drives the story forward.

SA: Many of the characters in your books are trying to prove themselves, too, aren't they? In fact, one book is called *The Proving Ground.*

EMA: Yes. In that one, Kevin risks his life in order to save a military base and the town that surrounds it, but also to prove himself—to his father, to the girl he admires, and to himself.

SA: What other books would you recommend to readers who enjoy reading adventure stories?

EMA: Some of my favorites are *On the Edge* by Gillian Cross, *So You Want to Be a Wizard* by Diane Duane, *Hatchet* and *The Voyage of the Frog* by Gary Paulsen, *Alanna: The First Adventure* by Tamora Pierce, *The Reluctant God* by Pamela F. Service, *Grab Hands and Run* by Frances Temple, *The Grounding of Group 6* by Julian Thompson, *Jackaroo* by Cynthia Voigt, and *Ghost Abbey* by Robert Westall.

4. SUSPENSE

D ANGER DOESN'T always require an unusual setting. Sometimes the familiar can suddenly turn threatening: a shadowy figure appears, a flood cuts off the road to town, someone fails to show up for an appointment. The tension builds. Worry becomes fear; fear becomes terror. Even favorite places can be the backdrop for a *suspense story* that keeps us flipping pages as fast as we can to find out if things will ever come out right for a character in trouble.

"Echoes Down the Rails" by Kristi Holl is that kind of suspense story. Jami is about to spend an hour doing something she loves to do: take charge of the Kate Shelley Memorial Park and Railroad Museum while Mom goes off to pick up Dad at his job. But there's a terrible storm, and Jami's little brother Blake disappears, and the tourist couple who were just through the museum might have been up to no good. Where's Blake? Will Jami be able to find him? Will she overcome her own fears in time to save him?

The railroad museum is a real place, the characters in this story are realistic, the time is now. But what you'll notice most about this story is the *suspense*. Jami's never quite sure what will happen next. And neither are we. . . .

Echoes Down the Rails

 KRISTI HOLL

" 'Bye, Jami! Keep Blake out of trouble."

"I'll try!"

Jami waved and hurried back inside the old train depot. Her mom volunteered at the railroad museum once a week, and Jami loved being left in charge for an hour while her mom picked Dad up from work. A couple of tourists had arrived at the remote park a minute ago. Jami just hoped her bratty brother stayed out of sight till she finished her little talk.

She nodded at the young woman in the pink floppy hat. "Welcome to the Kate Shelley Memorial Park and Railroad Museum."

The wind suddenly gusted, blowing brochures and postcards across the depot floor. Jami scrambled to gather them up. Dark scudding clouds outside deepened the indoor shadows.

Jami cleared her throat and started again. "This museum is on the exact site where fifteen-year-old Kate Shelley came to the Moingona depot on a wild night of storms and floods. The date was July sixth, eighteen eighty-one. Overnight this Iowa girl became an internationally known railroad heroine."

Jami pointed to the wall portrait that showed Kate as a young girl. Her brown hair was pulled back tight, and she gazed out of brooding, deepset eyes.

"Jami, there's a tornado!" Four-year-old Blake stumbled into the depot and zoomed from window to window. "Look at the clouds!" A cape made from his tattered baby blanket flew out behind him.

"Shhh," Jami hissed. "There's no tornado." She stood up straight and tried to remember her speech. "On that famous night in eighteen eighty-one, cloudbursts turned Honey Creek into a raging torrent and washed out a bridge near Kate's farm. Disaster struck when a locomotive didn't notice in time and plunged into the river."

"Boom!" Blake yelled. "No more train."

Jami sighed. "Be quiet, Blake. These people didn't come to hear you."

"Oh, that's all right." The young woman bent down to Blake's eye level. "If I had a little boy, I'd want him to be just like you."

Blake batted his eyelashes at her, then stuck out his tongue at Jami.

Fuming, Jami raised her voice. "Kate Shelley knew that the heavily loaded passenger train due soon must be halted. By a back route, she got to the rail line where it crossed the Des Moines River. On hands and knees, she started out in the raging storm over the six-hundred-seventy-three-foot-long trestle bridge. That's longer than two football fields." Jami's stomach tightened painfully at the very idea. "Kate's only light came from lightning flashes. The wooden railroad ties were spread too far apart, so she clutched a skinny rail to get across. She could easily have fallen through to the river below. After arriving on the other side, she ran another half mile here to the Moingona depot and sounded the alarm."

"How brave!" the young woman exclaimed. "I could never do that."

"Jami couldn't either," Blake piped up. "She can't even climb to the top of our hayloft without puking."

"That's *it*. Go outside, Blake. Wait for me in the passenger car."

Blake saluted, whipped his cape across his face like a bandit, then dashed out the door.

The mustached man glanced out the window. "The storm's blowing up fast. I'm most interested in the old passenger car. Could I go through that now?"

"Sure." Jami handed him a copy of the latest *Trail Tales* published by their county historical society. "Enjoy your visit."

After they left, Jami shut all the depot windows, straightened the pamphlets, and turned out the lights. Fighting the wind, she yanked the door closed behind her. Overhead the flag fluttered and snapped in the wind. At the antique passenger car, she climbed aboard. The young man and woman were near the front, examining the washroom and sitting room. Blake was nowhere in sight.

"Excuse me, have you seen my little brother?"

"He was just here." The woman toyed with yellow sunglasses that hung around her neck. "He said something about playing Kate Shelley on the real bridge. He offered to show us."

"Oh, no." Jami pivoted and jumped down to the ground, then ran for the bridge site about a block away. The only things left from the original bridge over the Des Moines River were the pilings. Blake always bragged that he'd climb up on those crumbling supports someday, just like Kate.

However, when Jami arrived out of breath at the bridge site, it was deserted. The wind whipped small whitecaps on the river. Waves pounded against the old bridge pilings.

"Blake! Are you here?"

When she scanned the area, she spotted something colorful snagged on a stick down by the water. She raced down to the river bank, slipped in the squishy mud, and snatched up Blake's frayed baby blanket. A numb feeling seeped through her.

Willing herself to stay calm, she studied Blake's footprints in the mud. Apparently he'd walked over to a grassy knoll near the pilings. The footprints stopped when they reached the weeds at the edge of the river. Had he returned? Jami couldn't tell. She stared at the gray water churning around the pilings and hated the thought that flashed through her mind.

Oh, no. He couldn't have.

"Blake! Blake!" She trembled uncontrollably.

Had he climbed up on the pilings? Had he lost his balance in the stiff wind and toppled into the water? The first raindrops hit the river just then, making polka dots that bounced and disappeared, then reappeared again.

Jami stuffed the corner of the baby blanket into her back pocket, then raced up the lane. Those two tourists would help her hunt for Blake. But when she rounded the last corner by the depot, the young couple's car was gone.

Jami stared at the empty parking lot. How—and why— had they disappeared so fast?

An uneasy fear washed over Jami, and the hairs on her neck bristled. That man had seemed so interested in the passenger car, but could it have been an act? Jami forced herself to breathe deeply and replay the incident. It was true: The man was very interested in the car, but not until Jami herself had sent Blake over there to play. Was there a connection? Was that why the woman had directed her down to the river, to get her out of the way while they kidnapped Blake?

Jami swallowed the cry of terror that rose in her throat. She'd heard about these child-snatching cases on TV, how kidnappers studied children's schedules, waiting to make their move. Anyone in town could have told them that Jami was alone with Blake at that hour every week. Jami bragged all the time about running the museum alone.

Blake could have been bound and gagged on the floor of that couple's car. He could even have been tied up at the back of the passenger car! The young couple had been free to take Blake as soon as Jami left on her wild goose chase to the river.

Suddenly one memory chilled Jami's blood. What had that lady said? She'd "love to have a little boy just like Blake."

Jami put a hand to her throat. What should she do? *I've got to call Mom. No, the police.*

Leaning into the driving wind, she ran to the museum to use the phone. Where was her mother, anyway? She should have been back with Dad by now.

Inside the dark depot, Jami reached for the phone on the shelf near the door. She grabbed the receiver and began to dial.

The phone was dead.

Her hand shook, and she dropped the receiver. She groped for the light switch. The lights were out too. Jami fought down the scream that rose in her throat, then headed back outside to check the power and phone lines. Either the storm was responsible—or the lines had been cut.

At the side of the building, she stared up to where the wire was strung across from the utility pole. When lightning flashed the next time, her view was crystal clear. The wire now hung loose, flapping in the wind.

Jami cringed at the trembling roar in her ears. The wind slapped her hair across her face as she climbed up on a barrel to get a better look. She squinted into the rain. The end of the wire was so frayed she couldn't tell if it'd been cut or not.

As she turned to jump down, lightning sizzled nearby. In that moment, Jami glanced toward the passenger car. A dark round bundle was up on top of it at the south end. What in the world?

Then she knew. "Blake!"

Lightning flashes outlined the twelve-foot-high car as Jami ran toward it, and its monstrous bulk looked a mile long in the dark. She found the metal ladder welded to the north end and clawed her way to the top. At the other end of the seventy-foot-long car was the dark unmoving shape.

"Blake! Can you hear me?" The wind whisked her words away. Blake didn't budge. Fear trickled down Jami's backbone like drops of icy water. What was he doing up there? Had he been struck by lightning?

Jami glanced down over the side of the passenger car and nearly fainted. It was like peering over the edge of the Grand Canyon. She dropped to her knees and, breathing raggedly, waited for her stomach to stop rolling.

Then she started across the top of the car. Intermittent flashes lit up the roof, then plunged her again into darkness.

One particularly close flash made her fling herself down and bury her head in her arms. "Come *on*. Keep going," she told herself.

Inch by inch, Jami crawled across the slippery metal car. It seemed like hours before she was even halfway to Blake. Gritting her teeth, she forced herself to keep moving. When she finally reached her brother, he was soaked to the skin and shaking. She grabbed him, and he clung to her.

"What are you *doing* up here?"

"I was p-p-playing Kate Shelley. The train was the b-bridge over the river. I yelled and yelled, but you didn't come."

"I couldn't hear you—all that wind and thunder." Jami hugged him again. "Let's get out of here."

As she turned, Jami's muddy shoe slipped. Her knee slammed into the metal roof before she landed on her stomach. Her foot and leg dangled over the edge of the car. She scrambled frantically back near the center. "Let's go, Blake. Be careful."

"I'll fall! Carry me."

"I can't walk on this thing! I can barely crawl." The very idea made Jami sick to her stomach. "Anyway, you got up here by yourself."

"But it wasn't dark and raining and slippery!"

Just then she remembered Blake's baby blanket tucked in her back pocket. "Here. Give me your hand." Jami tied one corner of the wet blanket around Blake's wrist. The opposite corner went around her own wrist. "Now we'll stick together, and you can't fall."

They started down the length of the passenger car. Jami's arms were so weak they barely supported her. Tiny streams of water ran down her face, into her shirt collar, and dripped from her nose and chin.

"Keep going. You can do it," she whispered to herself. Finally she reached the ladder. Looking over the edge, she was immediately dizzy. She closed her eyes and counted to ten.

Then she untied her wrist and climbed halfway down the ladder. Blake slithered down to her backward, and from there she guided him to the lowest rung. As they jumped the last three feet to the ground, headlights swung into the parking lot. Jami was leaning against the passenger train when her parents jumped out of the station wagon.

"Mom! Dad!" Blake yelled, running to them. "Guess what Jami did!"

Jami's knees buckled, and she slid to the ground. Thank goodness her parents were there. She knew they'd be grateful for her quick thinking in the thunderstorm, but no one would ever know about the bigger storm, the one that had raged inside her up on that train roof.

Jami was pushing her dripping hair back when a movement at the side of the depot caught her eye. She blinked once, then twice, not believing her eyes. A girl her age, in long bedraggled skirts, stood in the shadows. Her wet hair was plastered to her homely face, and she stared out of dark, deepset eyes. Jami gasped. She'd know that face anywhere. She'd stared at it hundreds of times in the museum.

Kate Shelley nodded. A small, tired smile transformed her homely face. Then, picking up her wet skirts, she turned in slow motion and disappeared into the stormy night.

Jami led out her breath as Kate faded away. Maybe she was wrong. Perhaps someone *did* understand what she'd faced and overcome that night.

Meet the Author

Kristi Holl started out as an elementary school teacher, and she wrote as a hobby while staying home with her small children. She soon learned that she loved being her own boss, setting her own work hours, and not having to go outside in those subzero Iowa mornings to go to work. Besides, she says, "Writing was fun! Where else could I get paid to make up stories?"

With a busy family of three biological daughters, an adopted Korean son, and two stepdaughters, Kristi Holl has always combined her writing with parenting. In her spare time, she loves to read, quilt, visit museums and historical sites, and hike. Her award-winning novels for young readers have been published in Denmark, Australia, and Japan.

❦

NOVELS BY KRISTI HOLL

Cast a Single Shadow	*Hidden in the Fog*
Danger at Hanging Rock	*Invisible Alex*
First Things First	*Just Like a Real Family*
Footprints Up My Back	*Mystery by Mail*
The Haunting of Cabin 13	*No Strings Attached*

Patchwork Summer	IN THE "JULIE MCGREGOR"
Perfect or Not, Here I Come	SERIES
The Rose Beyond the Wall	*A Change of Heart*
Let Sleeping Ghosts Lie	*A Tangled Web*
	Trusting in the Dark
	Two of a Kind

More about "Echoes Down the Rails"

KRISTI HOLL: I like to use real places for my stories. I like to visit the actual setting and spend time there. It helps me visualize the story events and gets my mind racing with ideas.

SANDY ASHER: So "Echoes Down the Rails" grew out of a visit?

KH: Yes, to the Railroad Museum and Kate Shelley Memorial Park in Moingona, Iowa. After reading about the true story of Kate Shelley's heroism during one terrible stormy night in 1881, I knew that I wanted to use the incident in a story. It had drama, strong characters, crisis, a riveting setting— all the makings of a suspenseful story. I used the kernel of that story in "Echoes Down the Rails." A thread of the past is woven throughout, and it meets the heroine in the present at the climax of the story.

SA: Iowa is the setting for quite a few of your books, isn't it?

KH: Several of my mysteries, yes. *The Haunting of Cabin 13* happens in Backbone State Park in northeast Iowa. *Danger at Hanging Rock* takes place at Effigy Mounds National Monument, a huge Indian burial grounds, also in northeast Iowa. And *Let Sleeping Ghosts Lie,* due out in 1996, is set in Iowa's Amana Colonies.

SA: How do you plan a story so that the suspense builds? How do you keep the characters—and the reader— constantly off-balance?

KH: At each turn in the plot I ask myself two questions: "What will the reader expect to have happen right now?" and "What totally unexpected thing can I have happen instead?" Whatever I choose has to be believable, though. Otherwise the reader will stop reading. I don't choose a bizarre twist of circumstances unless I can make it believable. Very often, I work in backward order. I think of something for the plot that is odd or strange or shocking, then work backward to plant clues and information that will make it believable.

SA: Can you talk about the importance of the two levels of suspense running through your story?

KH: The obvious level of suspense is about Jami fighting to save her brother. This is the basic conflict and holds the story together. But the second level—Jami battling her own fears—seems necessary, too. It makes the reader care more about Jami, and it gives depth to the story. The heroine can't succeed in solving the main story problem unless she also finds a way to overcome her "fatal flaw."

SA: Do you have any favorites among other mystery/suspense writers?

KH: Mary Downing Hawn and Joan Lowery Nixon. There are many types of stories that fall under the "suspense" label. The type I enjoy writing the most (and reading!) are the kind that could really happen—in real places to real people like me.

5. DETECTIVE STORY

*D*ETECTIVE STORIES come in a variety of shapes and sizes. But they all depend on a detective who solves a crime logically and systematically—by gathering clues, interviewing suspects and witnesses, and analyzing evidence until the guilty party becomes obvious.

Crimes, criminals, and detectives come in a variety of shapes and sizes, too. Sherlock Holmes is probably the most famous adult detective in the world, even though he's a fictional character created by Sir Arthur Conan Doyle. Nancy Drew and the Hardy Boys are teenagers who've been solving mysteries for many years, to the delight of countless readers. The crimes they deal with are serious: robberies, kidnappings, poisonings, and so on.

In our next story, Gary L. Blackwood introduces an even younger detective, one who has no crime-solving experience at all. Armed only with her well-read copy of *How to Be a Detective,* Heather bravely sets out to uncover the truth about "Who Waxed Mad Max?"—a Halloween prank that has her big brother grounded. Unfairly? Maybe. Maybe not. The answer doesn't come easily. As in all detective stories, false clues and unreliable witnesses lead detective and reader astray.

Like all our stories so far, "Who Waxed Mad Max?" is realistic and contemporary. Like "Alligator Mystique," it's got a great sense of humor. But most of all, it's got Heather, and no matter how new she is to the job, she makes this a *detective story.*

Who Waxed Mad Max?

❧ GARY L. BLACKWOOD

I was in the kitchen, sorting through my Halloween goodies, when I heard Dad and Nick arguing. I couldn't tell what it was about. Then the door to Nick's room slammed.

I waited awhile, to let Nick calm down, and then I knocked on his door.

"Yeah, what?"

"It's Heather. You want to trade some candy? I got a bunch of licorice."

"I guess. Come on in." He was lying on his bed, still in his devil costume; the red fabric was wet.

"You better get out of that stuff," I said, "before you catch cold."

As usual, he ignored me. "Nobody ever believes me," he said.

"About what?"

He rolled over with a groan and started thumping his wastebasket with one soaked sneaker. "Max McCracken called Dad and said I waxed his windows."

"Did you?"

"No!"

"Just asking. What makes him so sure it was you?"

"He says he heard me telling you I was going to get even, as we walked off."

"Well, you did. When all he gave us was a Hershey's Kiss apiece, you said it rotted, and somebody ought to wax his windows good."

"That doesn't mean I *did* it! Look, why don't you go tell Dad it wasn't me? He'll believe you."

I sat on his desk, next to his orange plastic bag of candy. "I can't do that, Nick. I was only with you about an hour. I don't know what you did after that."

Nick kicked the wastebasket over. "See? Nobody ever believes me!"

Though I wasn't sure it was exactly true, I said, "I believe you."

"A lot of good that does me. Dad doesn't. So I have to either clean all the wax off, or stay in my room until I do."

"You want me to help you scrape the windows?"

"You wouldn't be much help, shrimp. Besides, I'm not doing it. I'll stay here until I rot before I'll clean Mad Max's windows."

I giggled. "Mad Max?"

"That's what we call him at the junior high. The guy's nuts. How he got the job as our custodian I'll never know."

"You know," I said, thoughtfully, "I've been reading this book called *How to Be a Detective.*"

"Yeah? So?"

"So, I bet I could figure out who did it."

He laughed. "Right, shrimp."

"You never think I can do *any*thing." I tried half-heartedly to whack him with a licorice whip.

He just caught the end of it effortlessly. "You can't." He eyed the rest of my licorice. "I'll trade you all my Sweetarts for those."

"OK." As I dug through Nick's bag, I came across a lump of red stuff and fished it out. It was a pair of wax lips—at least it used to be. Now it was just a blob of wax, half worn away, as if somebody had been . . . had been waxing a window with it.

I glanced at Nick. He wasn't paying any attention, so I slipped the wax lips into my sweater pocket. "Not to worry," I said. "Inspector Heather is on the case."

He laughed again.

It was just as well that Nick had to stay in his room; the next morning he had a cold so bad, he sounded like Darth Vader.

I stuck *How to Be a Detective* in my purse, along with a notebook and pen, and headed for Mad Max's house to look for clues. As I went out the front door, Rowdy Alumbaugh came up the walk, in his usual outfit of baggy sweatshirt and torn jeans. "Hey, twerp," he said, around his usual mouthful of bubble gum. I guess I should have been flattered that he noticed me at all.

"If you're looking for Nick," I said, "he's grounded."

"Until when?"

"Until indefinitely."

"What'd he do, kill somebody?"

"My dad thinks he waxed Max McCracken's windows."

Rowdy stared at me for a second, probably the most attention he'd ever given me. "What makes him think that?"

"Mad Max called him and said so."

Rowdy made a disgusted face. "What a jerk. He's always getting kids in trouble. You know what he did to me? He saw me sticking gum under a table in the cafeteria, so he makes me scrape every piece of old, dried-up gum off every table in the place. The guy's mental."

Just what I wanted to hear, considering I was on my way to the guy's house.

Rowdy shrugged. "Well. Tell Nick I came by." He shuffled off, but turned to add, "Tell him I'm sorry. About the grounding, OK?"

Mad Max McCracken's house was the creepy sort of place most trick-or-treaters shun. For a janitor, he didn't keep his home up very well. The porch threatened to part company with the house any day; the curtainless windows were so dirty, the wax didn't make much difference.

Hoping Mad Max slept late on Saturdays, I stepped softly across his balding lawn. It took me a minute to decipher the words scrawled in big letters across his front window. They were printed backward, so they could be read from the inside: MAD MAX IS ME! Well, that made no sense at all. It could have been MAD MAX IS MEL, but that made even less sense. Still, it was a clue. I copied the message in my notebook.

Then I parted the half-dead bushes and peered at the muddy ground below the window, looking for footprints. There were plenty. Just as it said to in *How to Be a Detective*, I tore a page from my notebook and pressed it on top of the nearest print. When I pulled it away, there was a perfect copy of the print, outlined in mud. I tucked the paper in the notebook and searched for more clues.

Right at the base of the foundation was a glob of something purple. I bent over the bushes, reaching for it. A sudden burst of high-pitched yapping just inches away made me jump and knock my head against the windowsill. "Ow, ow, ow!" I staggered backward, holding my head. "What in the world—?"

It was Mad Max's schnauzer, barking and leaping at the windowpane. I flapped a hand at him. "Ssssh! Shut up, you dumb dog!"

It was too late. The front door opened, and Mad Max emerged. He was unshaved; his gray hair stood up in all directions. He wore a holey T-shirt and bib overalls; his slippers looked as if the schnauzer had tried to have them for lunch.

"What do you want?" Mad Max bellowed.

What I wanted was to run. But that wasn't what a good detective would do. A good detective would ask questions. "I—I—I was looking for clues," I mumbled.

Mad Max scowled at me and scratched the holey T-shirt. "Clothes?"

"Clues! To find out who waxed your window."

He snorted and spat over the railing. "I know who done it. Your brother."

"He says he didn't."

"Then he's lying. I seen him. Get on out of here, now."

I would have been happy to. But my investigation wasn't complete. "You see—you saw him actually waxing the window?"

"Shut up!" Mad Max yelled. I almost bolted, until I realized he was talking to his noisy dog. "Honey there was barking"—I had to squelch a snicker; his dog's name was *Honey*?—"and I come out to see what was going on, and I seen your brother running off."

"You're sure it was him?"

"He had on a devil suit, same as when you come to my door."

I made a note of this. "Well, thank you for your time, Mad—Mr. McCracken."

For the next hour or so I went around the neighborhood, asking kids if they'd seen anybody wearing a devil suit like Nick's the night before. Somebody said Zack Tommey had one. My first suspect. Aside from Nick, of course. Zack was known for his stupid sense of humor, so he made a good suspect. I stopped by his house, but nobody was home. My first dead end.

When I went home for lunch, Nick was still in his room, and still hacking and sneezing. Pretending I was looking for a piece of candy I'd dropped, I hunted around under his bed until I found his sneakers. The treads were packed with mud. I unfolded the print I'd made and held it up to the shoe. A perfect match.

"What are you dooig under dere?" Nick rasped.

"Nothing." I stuffed the paper in my pocket and slid out. "Nick. Where'd you go last night after I came home?"

"Hey! Dod you stard on me, doo! I'm innocend!"

I wanted to believe him. He was my brother. But the evidence was against him.

The book said not to jump to conclusions, to let the clues stew in your brain awhile. So I did.

I was giving Zack Tommey a call that evening when Rowdy came by again, claiming that his Halloween sack had gotten switched with Nick's—and that his had more candy in it.

I tailed him silently to Nick's room and stood with my ear to the crack of the door, hoping Nick would let something slip.

"Hey, Nick," said Rowdy's voice. "How's it going?"

"Lousy. I'm grounded for someding I didn'd even do!"

"Yeah, I heard. I feel really bad about it, too."

"I'll bed. Listen, close de door, okay?"

"Sure."

I flattened against the wall as Rowdy crossed to the door and pulled it shut. My little finger got pinched in the crack.

A real detective probably wouldn't have yelled. But I wasn't a real detective yet. "Agghhh!"

"What the heck—?" Rowdy flung the door open. "What are you doing out here?"

"Nothing." The word came out funny because I was sucking my finger.

Rowdy shook his head. "Nick, I think the twerp's going mental."

He started to shut the door, but I grabbed it with my good hand. "What did you just say?"

"I said you're mental." He blew a wimpy bubble with his gum in my face.

"That's what I thought. Open your mouth."

"What?"

"I said, open your mouth and let me see that gum." He looked at me like I really had gone over the edge, but he opened his mouth. "Just as I thought," I said. "Purple."

"It's grape. So what?"

"So you were the one who waxed Mad Max, that's what."

Nick sat up in bed. "How do you figure?"

"It all adds up. The wad of gum under the window. The message." I flipped open my notebook. "What I thought was an exclamation point was the start of an N. MAD MAX IS MENTAL. Only you didn't get to finish it, because Mad Max scared you off—so fast that you grabbed the wrong candy bag. Nick didn't do the waxing, but he was there. Right so far?"

Rowdy looked down at the floor sheepishly. "I was afraid if I confessed, your dad would call my dad. And my dad's a lot stricter than yours."

"So you let my brother take the rap? Some friend." I

turned to Nick. "Why didn't you just tell the truth? Why'd you cover for him?"

Nick just shrugged. But I knew the reason. It was the same reason I'd stuck by Nick, in spite of all the evidence. Loyalty, I guess you'd call it.

"If you need to borrow a scraper," I told Rowdy, "we've got one."

"Naw," he said. "I'll take care of it. I'll just get my candy."

"Not until I get my fee," I said.

Rowdy gave me another of those "you're mental" looks. "Fee? For what?"

"For breaking the case."

Nick laughed hoarsely. "She's right, Rowdy. Give her some of your lood." He reached into his own bag, pulled out a fistful of goodies, and held them out to me. "I guess you're good for somedhing after all, shrimp."

I smiled smugly, and turned my penetrating detective's gaze on the candy. "There better not be any licorice in here."

Meet the Author

Gary L. Blackwood grew up in western Pennsylvania, where, he says, he spent "half my time wandering in the woods, and the other half wandering in books."

He sold his first children's story while still in college. Since then, he's worked as an advertising artist and copywriter, army sergeant, bookstore clerk, library assistant, loader of meat trucks, handyman, and "sometimes even a writer." He lives with his wife and two children in the foothills of the Ozarks and still adventures outdoors and in books.

Gary L. Blackwood is a playwright as well as a novelist.

Novels by Gary L. Blackwood

Beyond the Door	*Time Masters*
The Dying Sun	*Wild Timothy*
The Lion and the Unicorn	

More About "Who Waxed Mad Max?"

SANDY ASHER: Tell us about the unusual way you began writing "Who Waxed Mad Max?"

GARY L. BLACKWOOD: It was the first time I'd consciously used the device of free association, in which you begin with a word chosen at random, then write down whatever other words or ideas it calls to mind. It worked. I started with, as I recall, the word *Indian.* That led to other words, including *mask,* which suggested *Halloween*—and all the rest followed.

SA: Is it true that mysteries have to be written backward?

GLB: I approached "Mad Max" pretty much the way I approach any story; I always have to have some idea of where the story's going before I begin, and that's crucial with a mystery. If the author doesn't know up front "whodunit," he can't very well plant the clues.

Every story of any kind has its equivalent of clues, things that make the reader look back at the end and say, "Oh, yeah, I should have seen that coming." In some stories, you *want* your readers to see it coming, so they can anticipate. But not in a mystery. If they figure it out too soon, it spoils the surprise. Ideally, they'll "get it" about the time the detective does.

SA: How do you decide what clues to provide and how to plant them?

GLB: Obviously, the clues can't be too easy, or your detective seems incredibly dense not to have deciphered them. Nor can they be so difficult that it would take a genius to piece them together. The toughest clue to plant in "Mad Max" was the wax message. It had to seem to make no sense but be part of a longer message that *did* make sense. At first, I had the message read MAD MAX IS MEN, but my twelve-year-old son immediately made the connection with Rowdy's favorite term, "mental," so I had to remove all but one stroke of the N.

SA: Heather does more than solve a mystery in your story. She gains her big brother's respect. Was that intentional on your part?

GLB: If the detective in a story doesn't have some personal stake in solving the mystery, then it's just a puzzle, not a story. In real life, each time we figure out the answer to some problems that plagues us, we learn something from it. So should the character in a story. Heather has two pretty strong reasons to want to dig up the truth—her desire to prove that her brother is innocent, and her desire to prove that she's not just a "twerp."

SA: What does this story have in common with the books you've written?

GLB: Like Tim in *Wild Timothy*, Heather is in the shadow of an older brother. Like Scott in *Beyond the Door*, she thinks that things can be worked out by using logic. And she's loyal, like James in *The Dying Sun*. Even though the books aren't detective stories, they contain many of the elements of a good mystery—things that keep the reader guessing.

6. ANIMAL STORY

THERE ARE basically two kinds of *animal stories:* those in which the animals think and talk as human beings do, and those in which they do not. Patricia Calvert loves both, but "Tug, in His Own Time" is an example of the second kind and seems very true to life.

In realistic stories like this one, animals maintain their silent, steady, somewhat mysterious natures. Caring for and working with such animal companions has a strong effect on the human characters; they are the ones who change and grow. "I learned about loyalty, patience, endurance, and about dying with dignity from the many animal friends of my childhood," says Patricia Calvert, "but I cannot say if they learned anything at all from me."

Even though Tug, the mule, and Webb, the boy who loves him, lived years ago, when tractors were just beginning to replace mules on family farms, we can easily understand and believe in their world. The hard work of growing up—and growing old—hasn't changed a bit.

Tug, in His Own Time
PATRICIA CALVERT

The barn was dim, silent save for the murmuring of pigeons in the loft. Webb averted his glance as he hurried past the new tractor. Pa might as well have driven that 1947 John Deere into the yard last week with a banner draped across it announcing, "So long, Tug."

Webb headed for the pen behind the barn. Tug would be surprised to see anyone so early in the morning.

"Can't make do with a one-hitch mule anymore," Pa declared at supper last night. "Oh, I admit that mule was a pullin' fool in his day, Webb, but now that we got the tractor . . . well, time's come to put Tug down." He tried to lighten the decision by joshing. "One thing about a tractor, son. You only feed it when you use it—darn ol' mule wants to eat every day, whether he works or not!"

But the only words Webb heard were those three, *put Tug down.* Short; simple; almost innocent. Spoken aloud, though, they were a death sentence.

The boy pushed his plate away, hoping Mama wouldn't fret, "Why, son, whatever ails your appetite tonight?" In her way, she loved Tug, too. Not that she'd ever worked him, or that she was overly fond of critters at all. She just knows what he means to me, Webb realized.

"I'll take care of it in the morning," Pa went on. "Then I'll go up to that north field. Bet I get it plowed in half a day. Think of it—doing in hours what it'd take Tug three, four days!" He sounded pleased and eager.

Webb studied the table top. "About putting him down," he blurted. "Let me do it, Pa."

He knew exactly how it was done. Two years ago, he'd been with Pa when Patsy, Tug's longtime companion, was put down after she broke her shoulder.

The .30-.30 would be loaded, would be held lightly behind Tug's ear. The deed would be clean—as clean as gunshot wounds ever were, at any rate. Tug would go down easily, without a cry. He might shudder once, as Patsy did, then his bright blood would drain away into the dark soil they had plowed together so often.

Neither Pa nor Mama seemed surprised by his request. "I figured you'd want to," Pa murmured. "You haven't lived a day on this earth but what Tug wasn't on it with you, Webb. He was only six, same year you were born, when I bought him off old man MacKenzie. But he's nineteen now, older in mule years than your grandaddy was in man years when he passed on."

Now Webb tightened his jaw. He didn't want to wrestle with comparisons between mule years and man years. Instead, he steeled his will for what he'd pledged to do, and opened the gate to Tug's pen.

The mule raised his head from where he dozed at his grain box. His forehead, once dark as charcoal, was haloed now with silver hairs. He nickered slowly, his long ears pricked forward attentively. There was something in Tug's glance that had always pleased the boy. This morning, the mule's eyes (dark brown, a pair of wells that seemed to have no bottoms) held no grievances against executioners.

Webb ran his palm down the mule's haunch. His coat was smooth and warm. When Tug shifted his weight, the boy felt muscles run like trout under the mule's hide. He clipped a rope to the halter that Tug wore.

"Let's you and me go down by the creek," Webb invited. He didn't want his words, or the way he said them, to give the impression there was anything unusual about the day.

"You always liked it down there," he reminded Tug. "Patsy too, remember?" He'd propped the rifle against the gate; he retrieved it as they left the pen. He didn't hurry. Why should he, when time, for all time, would so soon be ended for Tug?

The wild timothy grass along the creek bottom was high as the boy's knees, and soaked his pants through with dew. Birds were beginning to call back and forth among the tops of maple and birch. The gloom of night had brightened to the color of ripe peaches along the ridge.

The rifle was loaded. There were two extra shells in his pocket. When Tug bent his long, silvered head into the timothy, Webb shifted the rifle to his right hand. The barrel was blue, and gleamed dully in the faint morning light.

There was a smooth, soft indentation behind Tug's left ear. Webb laid the muzzle of the rifle against that spot. Done right, the deed would require only a single shot. The trigger felt eerily smooth beneath the boy's finger.

Slowly, Webb lowered the rifle. He ejected the shell into his palm.

"C'mon, Tug," he said, and led the mule across the creek. Together, they headed for the clearing near the old quarry, a place he often came himself to lie on his back and watch the clouds. If you were an only son, your three baby sisters buried long ago, if you lived far from neighbors—why, then a boy learned quiet ways to pass his time.

The grass in the clearing wasn't as thick as beside the creek. Webb staked the tether rope so Tug could graze in a circle of about twenty feet. Later he'd bring down some hay, and that dented old bucket for water. A few oats, too, though not enough to make Pa suspicious.

Webb headed back to the barn. He looked back once through a thin screen of trees. He returned the shell to its chamber. Tug was grazing but raised his head when the rifle was discharged into the air. The mule didn't bolt like a fool horse would have, and across the distance that separated them, Webb was sure Tug exchanged a knowing look with him.

At breakfast, no one inquired about the deed. The gunshot had been heard; it was taken for granted, Webb knew, that he'd carried out his pledge. There would be no need to bury Tug; it would take only a few days for his carcass to be picked clean by foxes, badgers, and skunks, just as Patsy's had been. But Webb was surprised that his heart felt sore and bruised, as if Tug were truly dead. He never imagined deception would be such a heavy load to carry.

Each evening, Webb made sure he prolonged his chores, making it easier to sneak away with a cupful of grain in his pocket, an armful of hay clutched to his chest. If he took the long way to the creek he knew he couldn't be seen from the house.

Once, Tug was lying in the clearing, flat on his side, as the boy approached. Webb's heart leaped up to think maybe the mule had died naturally, that his pledge wouldn't need to be fulfilled after all. But Tug was quite alive, and got up—stiffly, slowly—and lipped the oats out of the boy's palm with a grateful sigh.

Webb sighed himself. "Oh, mister, if only there was another way. . . ." But of course there wasn't.

Five days after Tug supposedly was put down, Pa came in early from the big field to the west. His eyes were black with consternation. Webb found himself hoping the tractor had broken down. That it had proved to be a piece of overrated machinery that would have to be hauled back to where it came from.

"It was my own doggone fault," Pa admitted. "Sure's I'm alive, I knew that field stayed wet where the spring comes up in the center. Got one wheel of that tractor buried up to its axle." He squinted through the window into the hazy Indiana distance.

"Worse, rain's on the way, making me wonder when I'll ever get the blame thing out. I'd ask Jasperson to give me a hand, but I know he's all tied up with his own field work."

Pa never liked to ask for help, always wanted to handle his problems by himself. *But Tug and me could help,* Webb realized.

He stirred uneasily under the weight of the secret he'd kept for more than five days. He told himself it wasn't as if he'd actually told a lie. He'd never come right out and said, "Tug's been put down, just like you wanted, Pa." But the truth was, Tug *was* alive and eating a cup of oats every evening! Webb swallowed hard, then took a deep breath.

"There's something I have to tell you," he announced.

Mama and Pa turned to him, astonished. What did they hear in his voice that made them both stare at him as if they'd never seen him before, as if a strange, unfamiliar boy had suddenly appeared in their kitchen?

"I didn't put Tug down," he said. There. Now they knew. He hadn't lied, but he hadn't been honest either.

His mother laid a flour-covered hand over her heart, leaving the imprint of five white fingers on her blue apron. His father's jaw dropped; he closed it with a snap that echoed in the quiet room.

"When I led him down to the creek, well, I just couldn't. So I took him to that clearing near the quarry. I figured to do it soon, though." His parents' eyes skewered him in place; Webb couldn't have headed for the door even if he'd tried.

"Let me go fetch him, Pa. You and me can go down to where the tractor's stuck. Give Tug a chance to pull you out."

"It's bogged down awful bad, son. Way I see it, it would most likely take Tug and Patsy together. Without her . . ."

"Won't know till we try," Webb heard himself point out.

After having been visited only at eveningtime, Tug seemed pleased to get company so early in the day. There was something so warm and glad in his trumpeting bray that Webb let himself believe everything might have a storybook ending. Every night, he'd dreamed how it would be: somehow, Tug would be given a chance to prove how valuable he still was; his death sentence would be revoked; he would live out his days belly-deep in timothy, to die later of something ordinary.

Pa harnessed Tug, and they went together to the west field. When the tow ropes were hitched onto the John Deere, Pa stepped back. "I'm not sure he can do it, Webb," he muttered skeptically. "Doggone tractor must weigh about—"

"Give him a chance," Webb insisted. He wished he could whisper in Tug's ear, *Done right, boy, might mean you don't get put down after all!*

Instead, he called simply, "C'mon, Tug." Tug leaned into the harness. Then, finding himself on spongy footing where all four hooves had a poor purchase, the mule shifted expertly a couple steps to the left. He leaned into the harness again, neck bowed, the muscles of his haunches bunched like knotted fists beneath his smooth charcoal hide.

A sound came up from somewhere in his barrel chest. It was one Webb had heard often, whenever Tug had an especially tough job to do—a clamping down of breath deep in his great lungs, a hardening of his heart for the task ahead.

"Tractor's stuck too bad," Pa warned. "Alone, Tug can't—"

"Let him try, Pa," Webb called back. Then to Tug he whispered urgently, "You can do it, mister, I know you can. Now, *pull!*" In his own heart, he knew Tug still had the will for such a challenge.

There was a sucking sound when the right wheel of the John Deere let loose. The tractor rocked once, twice, then Tug hauled it, inch by terrible inch, onto a lip of solid ground.

"Unhitch him," Pa hollered, "and I'll start the tractor up!" Moments later, its engine making a *whumpety whump, whumpety whump* racket, the John Deere made its way to higher ground.

Webb turned to Tug. The mule stood with lowered head and half-closed eyes. His breath came in shallow little puffs, not the great blowing-out sound the boy was accustomed to hearing. Tug seemed mildly surprised, as if he'd just solved a riddle that had been puzzling him.

The mule swayed, seeming to brace himself against a hard wind, though not a breeze lifted across the half-plowed field. Webb watched him go down. Slowly. Easily. First to his knees, the way any four-footed animal such as a horse or cow goes down. Then, his back end. Last, his shoulders and haunches flattened, neck laid straight out. Tug moved his head once against the earth, and seemed to relish its sweet, familiar freshness. Webb saw the tender lining of Tug's nostrils were flecked with droplets of bright, frothy blood.

Webb knelt beside him. "It's all right, mister!" he called. "You did it, Tug. You did it. . . ."

The mule's lashes were silvery brushes against his face; Webb saw forgiveness in those brown eyes, and a tranquil regard for the day, the moment. The boy bent close, laid his cheek against the mule's. *Oh, Tug, if only you could speak. . . .*

Webb felt Pa kneel beside him. "Well, I'll be," he heard his father murmur. Pa laid two fingers beneath Tug's jaw. "Didn't I tell you he was a pullin' fool, Webb? Tugged on that tractor so hard his big old heart just broke."

"He went in his own time," Webb whispered, partly to Pa, mostly to Tug. His own recent deception weighed more lightly. Now there was no need for a putting down. This way, Tug had a chance to die the way he'd always lived, to fit his short, tough name right to the end.

Meet the Author

Patricia Calvert's parents were readers and storytellers. "So, perhaps it's not an accident they would produce a child who wanted to carry the process one step further," she says, "to publish books that others might read. But it took such a long time! Alas, I had some sort of reading disorder (no one seemed to know exactly what it was, something similar to dyslexia, perhaps), and I wasn't reading well until I was in the fourth grade. Yet by fifth grade, I had started to write clumsy tales about white tigers in the jungles of Africa, coal black stallions on the sands of Arabia, amber-eyed wolves in the wastes of Siberia—none of which I knew anything about at all!

"It was several years before I heard someone say, 'Write about what you know,' and when I finally heeded that advice, the stories seemed almost to write themselves. I became at last what my parents had been before me: a dreamer and a teller."

BOOKS BY PATRICIA CALVERT

NOVELS
Bigger
Glennis, Before and After
Hadder MacColl
The Hour of the Wolf
The Money Creek Mare
Picking Up the Pieces
The Snowbird

The Stone Pony
Stranger, You and I
When Morning Comes
Writing to Ritchie
Yesterday's Daughter

NONFICTION
The American West: Great Lives

❧

More About "Tug, in His Own Time"

PATRICIA CALVERT: Those of us who have been lucky enough to share our lives with animals are certain that we are richer for it. Three horses played big roles in my life—Redbird, Smoky, and Lady; dogs such as Bruno, Pepper, and Peaches also were more important than ordinary words can tell. Nor do I want to forget the special cats in my life—Agammemnon, Two Bits, and Alice.

SANDY ASHER: Horses, dogs, and cats. So—what made you decide to write a story about a mule?

PC: A few years ago a friend of mine gave me a copy of a popular magazine that included an article about mules. The more I read, the more interesting mules became to me, and—as all writers are prone to do when they accidentally stumble across something that grabs them and won't let go—I said to myself, "Someday I'll write a story about a mule." Someday finally arrived, and I named my mule Tug—a short, sturdy name that, to my way of thinking, summed up this animal's distinctive physical and psychological characteristics. Before the story was finished, I felt I knew Tug as well as if he'd belonged to me, rather than to a boy in Indiana named Webb.

SA: "Tug, in His Own Time" has a great deal in common with the books you've written. What similarities do you see?

PC: The story has three things in particular in common with nearly all my other fiction: first, it is about an adolescent character who is at a turning point or crossroads in his or her life; second, the character lives in a natural setting that includes woods, streams, fields, and open sky; and third, the closest companion the main character has is an animal. What happens in the story—to the human character and to the animal—changes the human character in a way he hadn't expected; he grows and changes, and afterwards is never quite the same.

SA: What other authors and books do you recommend to readers looking for more animal stories?

PC: The list of good books about relationships between humans and the animals in their lives is so long!—and I'm reluctant to leave any of them out. However, among my personal favorites I must mention *Call It Courage* by Armstrong Sperry, *The Midnight Fox* by Betsy Byars, *Thunderhead* by Mary O'Hara, and *The Yearling* by Marjorie Kinnan Rawlings.

7. HISTORICAL FICTION

REALISTIC STORIES don't happen just in modern times. "New Day Dawning" by Joyce Hansen is an example of *historical fiction,* a realistic story set in the past. Historical fiction allows us to travel back in time and experience life long ago as if it were actually taking place right in front of our eyes.

The events and settings in historical fiction are based on fact. Sometimes the characters are, too; fictional tales have been woven around such well-known figures as the heroic Joan of Arc and the outlaw Jesse James. Often, though, both the characters and plot are invented, as in "New Day Dawning."

The big challenge for a writer of this genre is to make the characters, what happens to them, and what they say, think, and feel *ring true,* even though the writer couldn't possibly have been around at the time to check it all out. Joyce Hansen will talk about how she does that, but first, journey back with her to South Carolina in the mid-1860s. The Civil War has just ended, and there's a new day dawning. . . .

New Day Dawning
~ JOYCE HANSEN

Sarah was careful of the thorns as she bent the stem of a deep red rose. She inhaled the flower's sweet perfume while watching several young men hurry through the gates and walk down the road. She knew that they were gone for good. Ever since the Yankee soldiers had come to the Thomas plantation in April to inform all of them that slavery and the war were over, people had been slowly leaving.

She picked another rose, turned around, and gazed toward the cotton fields, still dotted with the figures of men and women tending the growing plants that would be ready for picking by July. Sarah faced the road again and saw the young men disappear around a bend. In the past, the hounds would have chased them down, and Master George Thomas himself would have ridden, along with the patrollers, after them.

"Hey, girl, what're you looking after?"

Sarah jumped slightly. She hadn't heard Solomon approaching her. "Three more hands just left," she said.

"Yes. I know." A satisfied smile spread across his round face. "Ain't it wonderful? Them boys could just leave without a pass and see what's on the other side of this hill." His large eyes, as round as his face, fastened on her. "When are you leaving, Little Missy?"

"Don't call me that. I have a name." Sarah threw her head back and walked quickly toward the house.

Solomon followed her. "I'm just fooling with you, Sarah. Don't go getting mad."

Sarah passed the row of live oaks lining the walkway and glanced at Mistress Emmaline's bedroom window. Emmaline Thomas closed the curtain and moved away.

Solomon saw her, too. "Look at her watching her used-to-be property head down the road."

They walked toward the kitchen at the back of the house. "What're you going to do?" Solomon asked.

"Don't keep bothering me. I don't know."

Sarah and Solomon were both fourteen years old and had been born into slavery on the plantation. No one, not even Solomon, who was like her brother, seemed to understand how painful it was for Sarah to make a decision to leave the only life she'd known.

As she and Solomon entered the kitchen, the sweet smell of a pecan pie and Mariah's round scowling face greeted them. Mariah, the cook, was Solomon's mother and a mother to Sarah as well. Sarah's own mother had died giving birth to her.

"Where you been, Solomon? You might be free, boy, but you still have to work. Go on and fetch me some firewood." Her eyes fell on Sarah next. "You too, gal. No one's going to pay you to pick flowers."

"These are for Mistress."

Mariah sucked her teeth. "Mistress ain't studying you. Hardly talk to you or any of us since we been set free."

Davis, the Thomases' most favored slave, sat at the table as he did every morning, eating a piece of corn bread and drinking a cup of tea before beginning his chores.

He smiled at Sarah. "Little Missy, how're you this morning?"

Only Davis could call her that, for it never seemed as if he were mocking her. He had named her Little Missy when the Thomases' daughter, Caroline, had died at the age of ten. Sarah was a year older than Caroline and had been her slave and playmate. After her daughter's death, the grieving Emmaline Thomas increasingly sought Sarah's company. And the young girl became her mistress's personal slave and companion.

Sarah slept in Caroline's bedroom instead of on a pallet on the floor at the foot of Emmaline Thomas's bed.

"Mariah, I'm going to take these flowers to Mistress."

"Is she sick or something? You better stay here and learn how to cook, so you can support yourself. Cooks always find work."

Sarah sighed. "But Mistress might be wanting me."

"She knows where to find you if she wants you."

Sarah's small, brown, oval face, as well formed and delicate as the roses she carried, hardened like a little rock. Ignoring Mariah, who continued to grumble, she entered the sitting room. She'd spent some of the happiest times of her life here, playing with Caroline on the window seat as the sun filtered through the lace curtains, or sitting on the sofa next to Mistress Emmaline, learning how to make lace.

She put the roses in Mistress's favorite china vase, arranging the flowers as Mistress had taught her to do, and made up her mind to go upstairs without waiting to be sent for.

Mariah's voice broke into her thoughts. "Sarah, come on in here and help me."

Sarah ignored her and walked up the stairs. Before she reached the landing, Emmaline Thomas called from her bedroom. "Sarah, you mind Mariah."

"But, Mistress, I have some beautiful roses for you. Make you feel better."

"Go on and help Mariah."

Sarah's eyes stung as if she'd been slapped. More hurt than angry, she ran back down the stairs and put the vase on the fireplace mantel. Mistress knew how much she hated working in the kitchen.

Without a word, Mariah handed her a large basket of peas. Sarah placed the basket on her lap and sat near the window looking out onto the yard and the fields beyond. She listened for every sound in the house, hoping that Mistress would call her—wishing that their life could be the way it had been in the past.

Davis stared at her sympathetically. "Missy, you have to decide what you're going to do with this freedom." His teeth were as white and perfect as his starched shirt.

"I guess I'm going to set here and shell peas till my fingers fall off."

"You go on, Little Missy." He laughed.

"If she knows what I know she better leave with me and Solomon," Mariah said.

Sarah opened one of the pods so hard the peas popped out and rolled on the floor. "Mistress say that people who leave their homes are starving on the roads."

Mariah put her hands on her hips and bent over Sarah. "Girl, you'll be a slave all of your life."

"I am not a slave. Didn't Master and Mistress say they'll pay us wages?"

Mariah rolled her eyes. "Fifty cents a week? Even someone as ignorant as me knows that that ain't no money to build a future with."

"Well, Master and Mistress say—"

Mariah interrupted her. "Stop all that Master and Mistress slavery-time talk."

Davis drained his cup and smiled handsomely at Mariah.

"So what should the child call her? Emmaline?"

"Call her Miz Thomas and him Mister Thomas."

"Well, it seems strange to say something different," Davis said. "We been calling them Master and Mistress for so long. Maybe it don't mean nothing—just a way of addressing them."

"Names do mean something," Mariah insisted. "And Master and Mistress mean slavery time."

Davis turned again to Sarah. "You didn't answer my question, Little Missy."

Sarah lowered her head over the peas as she tried fighting back panic and tears.

Mariah spoke to the top of Sarah's head.

"Sarah, I held you in my arms when you was a baby and your mother died. You are the same to me as Solomon, my own flesh. I held you in one arm and Solomon in the other. You won't ever have a new life if you stay here and live like you did in slavery. Come with us."

Sarah couldn't tell her that she never felt like a slave, especially when Mistress was teaching her how to make lace and to quilt and was even beginning to teach her how to draw.

"Sarah, me and Solomon are leaving for Charleston. There's a freedmen's school there. They even have black teachers from the North. It's wonderful to just think about! My son's going to learn how to read and write and I can get work as a cook and make more than fifty cents a week. I'm going to get some land, too." She plopped down in the chair as if the excitement of her plans had worn her out.

"I'm leaving too, Little Missy," Davis said. "Going to Virginia to find my son and his mother. They lived on the Williams farm and was sold away five years ago."

Sarah was so surprised that she found her voice. "You have a wife and child?"

She never realized that Davis had a life that went beyond serving George Thomas. He had been given as a wedding present to the Thomases when they'd married thirty years ago and Davis was ten years old. He was a reliable and faithful slave—as polished and tasteful as the Thomases' fine china and silverware. Davis, with his slight bows, knew how a table should be set, how a master should be dressed and a household should be run.

"It was a slave marriage," he explained. "But I'm going to find them, and we're going to have a real marriage by a priest."

"How do you know where to look?" Sarah asked, forgetting her own problems for a moment.

"I have the name of the family they was sold to in Richmond. I'll find them if I have to walk the whole state of Virginia."

"You see," Mariah said, and shook her finger in Sarah's face. "Nobody is staying. It's a new day dawning."

"But Master and Mistress always treated me good."

"They treated all of us good. They also treat their expensive furniture good. And treat their cows and horses good, too. Paid a lot of money for them, and for us, too. Would you abuse something you paid good money for?"

"We're not property now," Sarah said softly.

"That's the point. Old George and Emmaline don't own your hide no more. There's no reason to take good care of you. You are on your own. You better learn how to take good care of yourself."

"But Mistress said that the freed people are sleeping in the woods and eating wild berries, and starving to death."

"She also said that Yankees had tails and horns."

"But she's going to pay us wages and she's going to teach me how to paint."

"Girl, you remember when Caroline took it into her head to teach you how to read and write?" Mariah's face softened into a slight smile. "And then you decided to teach Solomon the two words you had learned, and Miz Thomas caught you? Gave you and Caroline a whipping and told her daughter it was against the law to teach a slave how to read and write. Do you remember that? Remember how you cried because you really wanted to learn?" She was silent for a moment. "If you stay here you'll never learn nothing except how to remain a good slave."

Before Sarah could answer, Solomon burst into the kitchen. "Hey, y'all, something's happening. Them hands all left the fields and is walking up to the house."

Davis stood up quickly, putting his arm around Solomon's shoulders. "Come on, son, let's look like you're helping me with a chore, so's we can find out why those hands are trooping off to the big house."

"Sarah? Sarah!" Mistress called from the sitting room.

"Well, she finally got out of that bedroom," Mariah mumbled, as she too headed for the yard to find out what was happening.

Sarah put the basket of peas on the table and rushed to the sitting room.

"Yes, Mistress?" Sarah said, and heard Mariah's voice in her head warning against slavery-time talk. "You want to walk in the garden?"

"No, I'm tired." The lines around her mouth were like two deep ditches.

Sarah pointed to the mantel. "I picked some roses for you."

Mistress did not look. Closing her eyes as if she were in pain, she asked, "Are you abandoning me, too?"

"No, Mistress."

Emmaline Thomas pushed a thin, gray strand of hair away from her forehead. "Sarah, don't try to fool me. Everybody has changed. Even Davis. How could he think of leaving us? I'm not surprised about Mariah. She always did have a mind of her own." Eyes still closed, she rocked back and forth slightly. "Why are they leaving, Sarah?"

"They're the same. They just . . . they just want to have a new life."

Emmaline Thomas frowned as though Sarah had said something foolish.

"What new life? They're leaving by ones and twos—a trickle, but one day, it's going to be a flood and they'll all be gone. But they'll be back here in a month, begging me and Master to take them in."

Nagged by the word *Master*, Sarah was silent.

"You know no other place but this one, Sarah. You'll end up living in some cabin with cracks in the ceiling, so that stars are looking down on you at night. You're not used to living like that."

Emmaline Thomas opened her eyes, and Sarah was shocked to see tears brimming on her lashes and then trickling down her wan cheeks. "Sarah, don't leave. Remember how you and Caroline used to play?"

The tears were painful for Sarah, bringing back a rush of memories of the days when Mistress and Caroline were her world. Tears welled up in her own eyes also.

George Thomas suddenly entered the room, his tall, bulky body dominating the space. "Emmaline!" he shouted excitedly. "The field hands are demanding that we put a school on the plantation, so their younguns can learn to read and write. If we don't do it, they'll leave us."

The flood has begun, thought Sarah.

Emmaline sat up. "What did you tell them?"

"I told them yes. I need those hands to bring in the crop, Emmy; otherwise, we'll lose everything. Oh, I'll open up the school for them. I'll even let that Freedmen's Bureau send one of them black northern teachers."

"Who's going to put up the school?"

"I'll supply the materials, and the hands will build it."

This was the first time that Sarah had seen George Thomas smile in a long while. He clutched his wife by her sagging shoulders.

"Oh, Emmy, if the hands stay, we can bring that cotton crop in and we won't lose everything. All they want is a school." He threw his large head back with its great mane of white hair, and laughed. "Emmy, you come on back to life. The world isn't dead yet."

He loosened his grip on her shoulders, and she gave him a weak smile. "Well, I don't suppose it'll do any harm. Those young ones are not much use in the field yet anyway."

Sarah didn't hear the rest of their conversation, for without warning, like a gift from heaven, the answer came to her, and she knew what she was going to do.

Emmaline Thomas's voice startled her out of her thoughts. "Come on, Sarah, let's take a walk, so I can see my garden."

As they strolled through the grounds bursting with roses and azaleas, Sarah asked, "If I stay here, am I free to go whenever I wish?"

"What kind of silly question is that? You belong here with us."

Sarah said nothing then or to Mariah and the others that evening. She wanted to make her decision strong in her own mind so that no one could change it. She could hardly fall asleep as she made her plans and strengthened her resolve.

She was up by dawn. She dressed quietly and sat on the side of her bed, waiting to hear her former mistress stirring. Finally, when she heard her walk across the room, Sarah knocked on the door and entered. "Miz Thomas, I have to talk to you."

Later, she ran down the stairs to tell the others the news. For a moment, though, when she saw Solomon, Davis, and Mariah sitting at the kitchen table, she felt as if her heart were splitting in two. "Morning, Little Missy," Davis said.

Sarah poured herself a cup of tea and sat down with them. "I made my plans," she said. "I told Miz Thomas that I would stay and work for her if I could go to the plantation school, too."

She braced herself for Mariah's eruption, but Mariah only asked quietly, "What did she say?"

"Said she didn't know why I wanted to learn to read and write; said it wasn't necessary for a colored girl to know such things. Said I already was a wonderful lady's maid. I told her that I wanted to be a teacher someday in a freedmen's school.

"And I told her I wouldn't abandon her if I could go to the plantation school. Then she said I could go to the school if I had a mind to."

Davis nodded his head. "You're growing up, Sarah. No more Little Missy, now."

"We can write each other," Solomon said.

Sarah looked at Mariah hopefully. "Now you can stay here, and Solomon can go with me to the plantation school."

But Mariah shook her round head. "Sarah, each of us takes freedom in his or her own way. I have to leave even if I only go around the bend to the Williams farm. If I stay here, I'll never feel free."

"That's right, Mariah," Davis agreed, tapping his forehead. "Freedom begins here, in our minds."

Sarah embraced each one of them. "Long as I'm free to go whenever I want, I don't mind staying a spell."

They were silent for a moment, listening to the whack of axes hitting the tree trunks as the bright sun burned off the last traces of morning darkness.

"Those hands have already started building their schoolhouse," Davis remarked.

"There's a new day dawning for all of us," Sarah said, "former slaves and masters alike."

Meet the Author

Joyce Hansen was born in the Bronx, in New York City, the setting of her first three novels: *The Gift Giver, Home Boy,* and *Yellow Bird and Me.* She grew up with two brothers in a large and close extended family and presently lives in South Carolina with her husband. "Though I have no children of my own," she says, "I feel that I have many children: my nieces and nephews, the children I teach, and the children I write for."

A graduate of Pace University, with a master's degree in English from New York University, Ms. Hansen has served as an intermediate school staff developer in the same New York neighborhood in which she's set several of her books. Until her recent retirement, she also taught literature and writing at Empire State College of the State University of New York. Her historical novels *Which Way Freedom?* and *The Captive* are Coretta Scott King Honor Books.

NOVELS BY JOYCE HANSEN

Between Two Fires	*Out from This Place*
The Captive	*Which Way Freedom?*
The Gift Giver	*Yellow Bird and Me*
Home Boy	

More About "New Day Dawning"

SANDY ASHER: Writers are often told to "write what you know." Obviously, you can't have experienced Sarah's story firsthand, so how do you "get to know" people, times, and places in history well enough to write about them?

JOYCE HANSEN: Through books, diaries, letters, and as many primary sources as possible. I try to get to know as much about a historical period as I can. With the characters, however, I've found that people have not changed over the years; that is, human nature has remained pretty much the same. People are good and bad; they love and hate; they want to be comfortable and secure. Characters in a story want something—those wants and desires, of course, are in the context of the times in which they live.

SA: But historical fiction is different from history. Does historical fiction have to be factually accurate, or can the writer just make up what he or she doesn't know for a fact?

JH: The historical background in historical fiction must be

accurate. The only fictional aspects are the characters and the plot. What the writer cannot document should be omitted. I got the idea for "New Day Dawning" from the research I've been doing on the Reconstruction period after the Civil War. I'm currently writing a nonfiction book about Reconstruction.

SA: So you write about history in both your fiction and non-fiction.

JH: I've written three books of historical fiction. Two of them, *Which Way Freedom?* and *Out from This Place,* are set in the South during the Civil War and the first year of Reconstruction. Sarah, in "New Day Dawning," is similar to the female character named Easter that I created in those two novels. I have another historical novel, *The Captive,* but the setting is New England right after the American Revolution.

SA: What other books would you recommend to readers who enjoy this genre?

JH: There are fine historical novels written by Walter Dean Myers, Scott O'Dell, and Mildred Taylor (especially her *Roll of Thunder, Hear My Cry*).

SA: Anything else you'd like to tell our readers?

JH: I enjoyed writing this story about Sarah and the other characters. I find that after many rewrites, the characters take on a life of their own. They begin to function without my help. When that happens, I know that the writing is going along well.

8. TIME-TRAVEL FANTASY

ANOTHER WAY to journey backward—or forward—in time is through *time-travel fantasy*. In this genre, some sort of magic or mishap allows characters to slip out of their day-to-day lives and experience adventures in a completely different time and place.

The lucky reader gets to go along—but only if that reader is convinced that the past or future is every bit as believable as the present. That means research on the writer's part, as well as imagination, and careful attention to details of life in the fantasy world being created.

Time-travel stories often begin with realistic characters and settings. In Pamela Service's "Family Monster," Urky is an ordinary teenager visiting Scotland with his parents. But he has an unusual first name, Urquhart—and that name links him to the castle lying in ruins on the shores of Loch Ness and to a most unusual creature named Tess. It is Tess's plight, along with her extraordinary powers, that take Urky and this story out of the real world and into the world of fantasy, where a simple but daring act makes all the difference for centuries to come.

Family Monster
~ Pamela F. Service

The moment he saw the girl walking toward him, Urky cringed. She had that dreaded trying-to-be-friendly look. He turned his eyes toward the blue-gray waters of the loch, but it did no good.

"Hi," she said, pushing back pale blond hair. Urky tensed, knowing what was coming next. "My name's Tess. What's yours?"

"People call me U.T.," he lied. It was worth a try. He *wished* people called him U.T.

That didn't seem to work either. "Oh?" the girl said, sitting beside him on the pebbly beach. "So what do the initials stand for?"

"My last name's Tredwell," he said flatly.

"And the U?"

He sighed. But what did it matter? In a few minutes they'd be away from this tourist trap and its nosy local girls and head back to the hotel. "It's for Urquhart. My mother's family name." Standing up, he grabbed a handful of pebbles and hurled them into the loch. "It's a stupid first name, and the nickname, Urky, is worse."

Laughing, the girl picked up a stone of her own and skipped it lightly over the glassy water. "How can you stand here, in the ruins of Urquhart Castle, and say that the name Urquhart is stupid? The first I saw you, I thought you had the look of an Urquhart about you. You should be proud of that name."

"Well, my mother is, and that's why I'm stuck with it. That's also why we're doing this stupid Scottish vacation. We've been at it for weeks, and I've seen all the battlefields, churches, and fallen-down castles I can stand! The only thing interesting about *this* place is that all the tourist stuff says there's a monster out there. Now, that would be worth seeing."

"Oh, so it's monsters you're wanting, is it?" Her Scottish accent was light and playful. "Well then, you're in luck."

"Oh, right. I suppose some faky monster model putts by here every hour to amuse the tourists."

This time it was Tess who threw an angry handful of pebbles into the loch. "They haven't sunk quite that low yet. No, I mean it's a full moon tonight. At Urquhart Castle on a full moon, you're almost certain to see the monster."

Trying to sound cool, Urky said, "You're kidding, right?"

"Wrong." Tess was playing with a necklace pendant that looked like a raisin clutched in a little silver claw. "You're staying up the Glen, aren't you? Come back here tonight and see."

"Is this place open at night?" he asked, trying not to feel or look even slightly excited.

"No, but I know ways in and out." Flicking back her hair, she flashed him an annoying little grin. "But you're probably afraid of monsters or maybe afraid that the ruins are haunted."

"Of course I'm not afraid!"

"Good. A real Urquhart wouldn't be. I'll meet you at the outer fence around midnight."

Before he could answer, his mother called from inside the ruined walls. "Urky! Time to go."

"See you at midnight," Tess said. "Unless you . . . what is the American term? Unless you wimp out."

Angry and, despite himself, a little excited, Urky joined his parents and headed toward the car. Is it true, he wondered, that Urquharts aren't scared of stuff like monsters and ghosts? This was one way to see. It also might be a way to see something more—that fabled monster. Of course, this could just be some trick the locals played on tourists. But if it wasn't, then maybe this trip wouldn't have been such a total boring bust.

Sneaking out of the bed-and-breakfast place after everyone was asleep proved easy. He left the door unlocked, the way he found it, though, as a city boy, Urky was surprised how nobody locked doors around here. Once outside, the route was plain even without streetlights. An enormous full moon had already risen above the wooded hill behind him, lighting the narrow road that skirted the shore of Loch Ness.

As he trudged along the grassy verge, Urky watched the ruins of Urquhart Castle looming closer and closer. The jagged outlines of broken walls and towers were silhouetted darkly against the moon-silvered waters of the loch.

Somehow the idea of the place being haunted didn't seem quite as ridiculous now. It was old, a lot older than buildings in America. There could be a few ghosts hanging around in the shadows. The thought slowed him a moment, but then he quickened his pace. Urquhart ghosts shouldn't bother him. He *was* family. And anyway, it was monsters he was after, not ghosts.

Tess was waiting for him at the fence, her long hair flowing like moonlight in the night breeze. Silently she led him through low, crackly bushes to a gap where they could slide under. By the time he was through, she was already trotting down the steep slope toward the castle on the headland.

It all looked different at night, with the tourists gone and everything a checkerboard of moonlight and shadow. The only sound was the wind as it rasped over pines and stone and slapped waves steadily against the pebbly beach.

Soon they were on that beach looking out at the loch, its wind-ruffled surface glimmering like tinsel in the moonlight. Urky stared and stared, but no dark dinosaurlike head broke the surface. The wind-driven cold began slicing through his jacket.

"So, where's the monster?" he asked at last.

Tess turned to him, the moon sparking emeralds in her eyes. "Maybe you'll see it soon. But I really brought you here for another reason."

All of Urky's city alarms went off. What did she want? To mug him, steal his money, passport, camera? He didn't have any of those with him. So maybe she'd kill him. He'd fight, but suppose she had a gang waiting in the shadows? Or maybe she wanted to sell him drugs or something.

He stepped back, crunching stones underfoot.

"Don't go. I just want you to steal something for me."

That jolted him. "Steal something? Here? What's here beside old rocks and tourist junk in the gift shop? Hey, do your own stealing. I'm out of here."

"No, wait!" She grabbed him, her sharp nails seeming to dig through his jacket. "I can't. But you can. You're an Urquhart. I wasn't sure I'd find one this time, not the way things have gone here. None of the local Urquharts will come near this tourist trap. Lucky for me, some overseas Urquharts are tourists."

Not a mugger or drug pusher, Urky thought. A crazy person. Big improvement. "Look, if it's family savings you think I can get at, we ought to be in a bank, not an open-air ruin. I'd better head back now."

"No! What I want is here. It's just not *now*. But you are an Urquhart, and this is the one night in the century when the past here is open to you. You can slip back and get what I need."

Sure, Urky thought. Just slip into the past and steal something. This kid was totally wacko. Better humor her. "Get what?"

"A bead. Just a little green stone bead. There were so many, they'll never notice you snatching one. Bring it back to me, and everything will be fine."

"Eh . . . right. A green stone bead. So where do I find this bead?"

"Step through that door at the bottom of the tower and climb up one flight of stairs. There'll be a bunch of people in the courtyard and lots of confusion. They won't see you well, so just go where the fuss is, wait for a chance to grab a bead, and hurry back here. That's all."

The tower, Urky thought. He'd been there this afternoon. The little door at the bottom opened onto the dungeon, and spiral stairs led to the main courtyard level. That'd put him well above the beach, separated from it by the outer castle wall. He could charge for the fence and be out of here before this lunatic realized he wasn't coming back with her imaginary bead.

"Right." He smiled blandly. "I'd better get on with it then."

"First take this." Slipping off her necklace, she dropped

it over his head. The chain and little claw hanging from it gleamed silver, but the black thing clasped in the claw still looked like a shriveled raisin.

"Now hurry," she said, pushing him toward the dark doorway. "You must do this while the full moon is still high."

A new thought struck him. "Hey, do you think you're a witch or something?"

She looked shocked. "A witch? Me? Of course not! I'm a kelpie."

So what was that supposed to mean? She was a vegetarian who eats kelp? If she was part of some crazy cult, he hoped it wasn't a type that waylays tourists and practices weird sacrifices.

Uneasily he stepped through the narrow archway. It was a lot darker and quieter in the old dungeon that it had been this afternoon. Misty gray light sifted through the door at his back and down the spiral stairs. There was no tourist babble, only a whispered shuffling—like mice. He hoped it was mice.

Quickly Urky stumbled to the stairs. He began climbing around and around in a tight, dark spiral until he almost fell through another door into the roofless room off the court-yard.

But now the room had a roof. And it had furniture and windows. Through those windows came voices—and bright morning sun.

Dazed, Urky walked across a woven rug to an open door and peered out. The sunlight made him squint, but he didn't miss the fact that the walls and towers, which earlier had been broken or mere foundations, were now tall and complete. He also couldn't miss the people in an angry yelling clump at the far end of the courtyard.

He stood there staring. Maybe that girl *had* slipped him some sort of drug. But surely everything looked too clear and real for that—even though the people were all dressed like in some historic movie. What were they going on about? They were sure upset about something.

Leaving the doorway, he cautiously walked in their direction. Nobody seemed to notice him, so he strolled more boldly to a shadowed wall near the edge of the crowd. For a moment, he thought he saw other figures there leaning against the stones, but when he looked directly at them there was nothing.

The action in front of him was far more attention getting. A tall, gray-haired woman was gesturing and screeching wildly. Beside her, a gray-bearded man stood glowering, beefy arms crossed in front of his chest. The crowd shifted slightly, and Urky saw who the woman was shouting at. He gasped.

It was Tess. Tess and a boy about his own age. There could be no doubt. It was the girl he'd just left on the moonlit beach. The long, pale hair, the catlike face, the green eyes, they were all the same. She was wearing a long, green dress and a bead necklace instead of a T-shirt and jeans, but it was her.

"She's not as pretty and innocent as she seems!" the old woman yelled. "She's a demon come to steal our grandson!"

"Come now," the bearded man said, "how could . . ."

"She's a kelpie, I tell you!" Urky started at the word, straining to hear better as the woman continued. "This little darling's a heartless water creature who changes form to lure young people to their deaths."

"That's not true!" the girl yelled back. "Your grandson and I are friends. I was lonely and I come here to play with him. I would never hurt him."

"But you cannot deny what you are! I and others saw you changing forms last night."

"Grandmother!" the boy cried. "What does that matter? She's my friend. She never causes any harm. Let her go."

"Let a monster like that go? No, she must be burned."

Frowning, the man laid a hand on the woman's shoulder. "My dear, surely if this sweet girl is the powerful creature you claim, she could just turn into a monster now and drive us all away."

"And what, husband, do you know about the mystic arts? I've studied them hour after hour while you've been off fighting useless wars. No kelpie can change shapes out of water. And to trap them forever in one shape, you need only remove their magic talisman!"

With that, the woman lunged forward, clutched the girl's necklace, and snatched it over her head. Squealing, Tess grabbed the necklace as it was whipped away. A short, violent struggle, and the string snapped. Green stone beads flew everywhere.

Some bounced toward Urky's wall. He leaped forward, grabbing one up. As he did so, he sensed other shadows peeling from the wall and doing the same, but he couldn't look at anything now except the drama before him.

Tess too was scrambling for beads, but suddenly the shrieking woman plunged at her with a knife. Jumping to her feet, Tess pushed through the crowd and out the gate that led to the beach.

Without stopping, she sped over the pebbles into the

water—deeper and deeper until her long, pale hair floated behind her like a shaft of sunlight. Like the glinting scales of a fish. A silvery fish that grew longer and longer until it became a sleek water beast.

The watching crowd screamed and pointed, but suddenly Urky realized the old woman was pointing his way.

"There are others here! With my art, I can see them. Don't let them escape with any beads!"

Brandishing her knife, she ran at him. For a panicky moment, Urky looked around for the tower he'd come through. Everything looked different when it wasn't in ruins. There—the tall, square one! He sped off, feeling other shadows rushing with him.

The confused, frightened crowd was blocking him. As he forced his way through, some of the people seemed to half see him and reached out. Ducking under groping arms, Urky dodged away, but the woman and her flashing knife had almost reached him. In a flock of shadows, he raced to the tower, the woman so close he could feel the breath of her screams.

Bursting into the room with the rug, Urky dashed toward the spiral stairs. Around and around he dropped through the tightening dark.

At the bottom, it was as if he had fallen into a well, a well of darkness and silence. There was no screaming or sunlight even in the distance. The trailing half-seen shadows were gone as well.

Trembling, Urky stepped through the narrow archway onto the moonlit beach. Tess was waiting for him, a smile glinting in her green eyes. Silently, he dropped the bead into her outstretched hand.

"I knew I could count on an Urquhart." Swiftly she lifted the pendant from around his neck. At a flick of her finger, the wizened black lump crumbled into dust.

"Once broken from the chain, they only last one hundred years," she said, popping the round green bead into the silver claw. "If I couldn't get a new one on this special night every century, I'd be stuck in one form forever."

Remembering the awesome creature he'd just seen, Urky stared at her. "Would being stuck as a girl really be so bad?"

Tossing back her hair, she laughed. "I'm a kelpie, a creature of land *and* water. I must be both to live. Were I cut off from the joys of the loch, I'd shrivel in misery. But now and again, I need to talk and play with other children. And sometimes too I take in the wonders of town—like movies and pizza nowadays. Besides, I need somewhere to hide when those meddling scientists looking for 'Nessie' get too close."

"So that old hag was wrong. You weren't going to lure her grandson away and drown him?"

"Of course not! Sometimes we played on land, sometimes on the water, but he was my friend. Young Urquharts have always been my friends, and every century one has been able to get me a new bead. It almost didn't happen this time, though, not with Urquharts avoiding the place." She grinned playfully. "Just think, without 'Nessie,' those tourist people would have to stop selling all that Loch Ness Monster trash."

Blushing, Urky thought of the plastic model he'd wanted. "I'm glad they won't."

"So am I!" She ran toward the water, then turned back to him. "I guess since you're a tourist, you'll be going soon."

"Tomorrow."

"Then come on. Let's play tonight!" She dove into the water, her hair trailing behind her like shimmering moonlight, like the silvery coiling body of a water beast. For a moment, Urky stood wavering on the shore. Then he plunged after her.

It was only a few hours, but it seemed timeless—clinging to her back, skimming over moonlit water; diving in a bubble of air to explore deep trenches and caves festooned with stone pillars and glimmering in their own green light; leaping and frolicking with fish and eels and creatures he couldn't name.

As dawn began fading the stars, he left her, climbing from the bay to sneak into his room and pack away his wet clothes. Lying in bed before sliding into brief sleep, he knew he would never forget any of it.

And he knew something else as well. "Urky" was a name to be proud of.

Meet the Author

"I was never a very athletic kid," writes Pamela F. Service, "but was always willing to trudge up the four flights of stairs to the children's room in the Berkeley, California, library. Once there, I usually picked up science fiction or fantasy, but one time I checked out *Mara, Daughter of the Nile* by Eloise Jarvis Mc-Graw. From that time on, I added history, particularly that of ancient Egypt, to my wildly mixed bag of interests."

Pamela F. Service earned her B.A. in political science from the University of California at Berkeley and an M.A. in African archaeology from the University of London. She has worked on archaeological excavations in Britain, the Sudan, and the United States. After settling in Bloomington, Indiana, with her husband and daughter, she found jobs touching both fields—she became a museum curator and was repeatedly elected to the city council. "I also began writing science fiction tales and sending them to publishers," she says. "After fourteen years, and only one published short story, came the first big acceptance—for a children's fantasy novel. Other acceptances followed. And I began to realize that though I enjoy the other things I do, and use them in my books, it is the writing that I really love."

❧

NOVELS BY PAMELA F. SERVICE

All's Faire

Being of Two Minds

Phantom Victory

A Question of Destiny

The Reluctant God

Stinker from Space

Stinker's Return

Storm at the Edge of Time

Tomorrow's Magic

Under Alien Stars

Vision Quest

Wizard of Wind and Rock

Weirdos of the Universe, Unite!

When the Night Wind Howls

Winter of Magic's Return

❧

More About "Family Monster"

PAMELA F. SERVICE: "Family Monster" came from a more personal source than most of my stories. My mother's mother was an Urquhart, and my parents had considered naming my brother Urquhart, but finally didn't, thinking the name too teasing-prone. I'd always thought that was too bad. It would have been an exciting link to the "family castle" on Loch Ness with all of its associations. Years later, when visiting Scotland to research another book, we stopped by those castle ruins and I fantasized about how such a link might be made real. This story is a result.

SANDY ASHER: Does time-travel fantasy require the same research as other forms of historical fiction?

PS: One of the tricky things about writing fantasy is believability. Because you are asking your reader to suspend disbelief for some aspects of your story, you need to try extra hard to make the other aspects totally believable or readers will dismiss the whole thing as nonsense. With time-travel stories, this means working on historical accuracy. I put in a lot of effort on researching the history and developing the period "feel."

SA: What does this story have in common with your books?

PS: I use time links in a number of my stories. *The Reluctant God* has someone from ancient Egypt coming alive in modern times, while *All's Faire* sends a modern kid at one of those Renaissance fairs back into the real Middle Ages. In *Vision Quest,* a charm stone creates a psychic link between a modern girl and a Native American of two thousand years ago, while family ghosts bridge a century's gap in *Phantom Victory*. The main characters in *Storm at the Edge of Time* come from the past, present, and future and pursue their quest in all three.

Old ruins crop up in lots of my stories—probably because of my love of archaeology. And a common theme seems to be having one or more fairly ordinary persons help some extraordinary ones with their problems.

SA: Will we ever meet Tess and Urky again—in a novel, perhaps?

PS: Originally I was thinking of this story idea as a novel, and I may still do that, but it would take a lot of rethinking to make the problems and the solutions complicated enough. Writing short is a challenge for me because I most enjoy the gradual development of plot, setting, and character that you have in novels. But a novel would give me an excuse for another research trip to Scotland!

Whatever the length, I am committed to time travel as an important genre. History is every bit as fascinating as the present—and there is so much more of it!

9. SCIENCE FICTION

To SOME readers, *science fiction* is a form of fantasy, an imaginative exploration of alien civilizations and futuristic events and technologies far removed from known fact. But to H. M. Hoover, author of "Just a Theory," "Science fiction is a story that *could* happen, if not now, then sometime in the past or future. Fantasy could never happen, much as we might wish otherwise."

However you look at it, good science fiction has a strong logical foundation. What is known—such as the human ability to travel through space—is extended in a carefully calculated way, perhaps to interaction between human space travelers and their counterparts on a populated planet of another solar system. "If the story takes place on an alien world," H. M. Hoover says, "the reader must be able to believe humans can walk there. Everything, from gravity and atmosphere to geology and life forms, must fit and be a part of that world if it is to ring true. In some respects, fantastic worlds must be more real, more logically detailed than straight fiction."

In "Just a Theory," logical thinking takes a humorous twist as aliens disrupt a group of young earthlings during a softball game.

Just a Theory
H. M. HOOVER

Invisible from the ground, the spaceship floated high above the softball field.

"There! You see!" Zebtor's antennae quivered with excitement as he pointed at the view screen. "A crude religious site! The white squares linked in a diamond-shaped path, the center mound, the net altar."

"So?" said Klive, unimpressed.

"Immature specimens of the dominant species are present on the site," Nuxsus observed.

"Which supports my theory!" insisted Zebtor. "The young perfect their skills in sites like these. When mature, they conduct the worship in the great stadiums of the major cities."

"You have no proof of this," Klive said. "For all you know they could be playing a game down there."

"Impossible," said Zebtor. "Surely even you can't dismiss the inherent symbolism expressed by the geometric patterns. And, primitive as they are, no game could provoke the fervor we've observed in the stadium worshipers. I'm going down."

And before his fellow scientists could protest, Zebtor degraved the ship to hover over deep right field.

Just then a high fly ball came soaring up and filled the view screen so aggressively that all three scholars ducked before the planet's gravity pulled the ball back down to earth.

"You glorb!" Klive swore. "You want to get us killed? Or noticed? What if that thing hit our shield and exploded?"

Nuxsus shook with fear but said nothing.

"Camera lenses make objects appear closer than they are," said Zebtor. He would not apologize for seeking truth.

On the ground, eight-year-old Justin closed his book and got up from the grass. He was frowning as he walked up the hill behind home plate.

Just as Paul hit the high fly, an odd shadow had raced across the field. Justin searched the sky for planes but saw none, not even vapor trails. At the top of the rise he shaded his eyes with his book. It wasn't his imagination; there was a patch of shade over deep right field—but no clouds or trees to cast a shadow.

The sky was milky blue, except for one spot where it seemed to . . . shimmer. When his eyes teared from sun glare, he squeezed them shut and watched the sun spots dance behind his eyelids.

By the time Justin saw him, Paul was halfway to second base while his teammates screamed and yelled and jumped up and down.

Chucky Michaels, the second baseman, was dropping back . . . dropping back . . . then turning and running. The ball zoomed over his head and didn't hit the ground until almost at the trees.

The shade moved toward the ball. The shimmering was near ground level now.

Paul sauntered from third to home, yelling insults at Bo Dai, the pitcher, and Chucky Michaels, and grinning broadly at the praise of his teammates.

Justin hesitated, then came down the hill to meet him.

"That was a good hit," he said.

"Like you'd know, butthead. Get out of my way."

Why did Paul have to be so mean? the younger boy thought. No matter what Justin said to him, Paul's response always hurt; an insult, or a punch on the arm, or the stomach—where bruises didn't show.

Justin had no interest in softball. He'd rather go home to do his homework and read. Or play with the little kids next door. But Mom said she couldn't impose on her neighbors, and he was too young to be alone in the house from the time school let out until she came home from work. So Paul had to baby-sit him to earn his allowance.

"Paul, did you see—"

"Move it!" Narrowly missing being called *out*, Paul gave Justin a savage push and touched home plate an instant before the ball slapped into the catcher's mitt.

Picking himself up from the ground, humiliated but persistent as a mosquito, Justin turned to Paul's teammates. "Can any of you see a funny shadow on the outfield? There, where the air's all shimmery?" He pointed.

"I told you to get out of here, butthead!"

"Please, I just want you to look—ooof!" Justin grunted with pain as Paul's quick rabbit punch hit him in the midriff.

"Get lost! Quit trying to get attention." Paul was yelling. "I'm sick of you! Mom and me got along just fine before you came. You're the reason Dad left us."

"That's not true! Mom said!" Justin was going to say—as soon as he had breath enough to talk again—but seeing the anger in his big brother's eyes scared him. Clutching his sore stomach he turned and walked slowly away, head down, trying to keep the older boys from seeing his tears.

"Pick on somebody your own size, Paul. He's just a little kid," Justin heard the catcher call.

"If you like the little wuss so much, you baby-sit him," Paul yelled back.

"My dad says little brothers grow up big and then they get even," said Bo Dai. "You better watch it."

"What's he going to do—hit me with a book?" Paul laughed at his own wit. Several of his buddies grinned, but others looked thoughtful, as if the idea of little brothers growing big wasn't entirely welcome.

Justin could hardly wait until that time came. When it did, he thought, he would hit Paul so hard . . . No, that wasn't true. He could never hit anyone. Not even Paul. So maybe he was the wuss Paul said he was.

Still carrying his book, he circled the backstop, heading toward the place where the air shimmered—away from humiliation.

Inside the spaceship, Nuxsus shifted nervously in his sling and said, "One of the natives may have noticed us. Are you sure you left the shield on?"

"Of course . . . my, it is a small one, isn't it?" Klive peered at the screen with his segmented eyes. "It appears to be wearing something over its skin. Coverings of some sort."

Nuxsus studied the screen. "Yes, doctor. It is wearing something. They all are. How curious. What purpose could that serve?"

"Ritual garb." Zebtor spoke with confidence. "If my theory is correct—"

"Note how its upper appendages end in four grippers and a pusher," said Nuxsus, ignoring his obsessive colleague.

"A crude but clever arrangement. See how the appendages curl to grip the object it carries."

"Object?" Zebtor tilted his body for a better view. The ship's camera brought Justin into extreme closeup. "A *book?* Yes! They have *books*! Plainly it's studying to become a priest. That's why it left the others—to meditate in private!"

"Calm down, Zebtor," Klive said sternly. "You're making wild assumptions to support a questionable theory."

"Or I'm right!" said Zebtor. "Sometimes one must risk one's entire scientific reputation on a hunch! An educated guess! Fly in the face of one's peers. For me to possess and translate that book would be an anthropological coup of cosmic proportions. It would make my reputation. . . ."

Before the other two could stop him, Zebtor activated the ship's Surface cue. The shuttle sank. Lights flashed. Alarms went off. Emergency gear dropped from ceiling compartments.

Lost in his own misery, Justin had to stop and blink and shield his eyes against a sudden gale of leaves, dust, and weed seeds blowing up out of the field. When he could see again, the mysterious shade was gone. In its place stood . . . what he was sure was a spaceship. He stared, openmouthed.

Higher than his house and shaped like a Hershey's Kiss, it stood on runners. It was covered with what looked like shiny brown glass and had blue markings, like writing, in a band around the bottom. Where the paper tail of a Kiss would be were multicolored antennae, like thick optical fibers. As suddenly as the ship had appeared, a large creature materialized beside the runners.

Seeing the thing, Justin thought: "Beam me up, Scottie." Scared as he was, he tried to smile a proper greeting.

In most sci-fi movies or books, aliens smart enough to

reach Earth were not only intelligent and kind but also reassuringly humanoid in form. This one looked like nothing he had ever seen.

It was huge, at least ten feet tall, and fat. It stood on many legs . . . or stiff tentacles, and had no arms. Its pinkish skin looked thick as an elephant's, with faint blue bumps all over. It wore only a spheroidal helmet as red as a Mercedes's taillight, but so thick he couldn't see the creature's head or face. If it had a head or face.

It occurred to Justin that he might be imagining this. He glanced back at the ball field. Everyone was running into the wooded park, except Bo Dai and two other boys. They were huddled behind the backstop, watching.

He looked back at the creature, hoping it wouldn't come nearer. It made bubbly sounds. He didn't know if it was talking or if the sounds came from it breathing in its helmet.

Maybe it was planning to capture him and take him to its world? Maybe for a zoo? He'd read a story like that once. Humans kept in a cage with a sofa, eating cornflakes while aliens pointed and laughed and threw peanuts at them.

The creature made more bubbly sounds and moved a leg. Justin wanted to run away but his feet refused to budge.

"Do you have . . . a translator?" he called, his voice squeaky with fear. In all the movies, aliens came equipped with computer translators that immediately understood any language, from humans' to alien reptiles'.

The creature bubbled again, then paused. It bent one of its legs up, reached behind itself, and brought out a purple mailing tube—or at least that's what the thing looked like to Justin. It held out the tube to him, as if offering him a gift.

"I can't," Justin started to explain, "I'm too scared to come near you—"

The book moved from his hand so unexpectedly he didn't even have time to try to grab it back. It simply flew straight to the alien, who caught it with a side leg and tucked it out of sight behind its back.

"You can't take that!" Justin said, horrified. "That's a library book. If I don't return it, I have to pay for it or pay ten cents a day! For life!"

The alien pointed the purple mailing tube at him. Justin threw himself flat on the ground and covered his head with his arms, expecting to get zapped—or whatever aliens did in real life. What if they did put him in a zoo?

Something hit the grass near his head. After waiting a moment and nothing happened, he risked peeking. There was a bright red stone sparkling in the grass where no stone had been before. The color was so rich and clear that he felt a crazy urge to pop it in his mouth and taste it.

Shifting light made him look up in time to see the alien dissolving into mist as its craft faded back into the shimmering light he'd seen before. A shadow flicked across the field and then all was as it had been.

Hearing the boys running toward him, calling his name, Justin reached out, closed his hand around the red stone, and put it in his pocket. The stone felt cool and oddly comforting to the touch. He decided he would hide it when he got home. If Paul saw it, he'd take it, just to be mean. And if that happened, Justin knew he'd never get it back.

He rolled over and sat up, shielding his eyes against the sun to look at Bo Dai, Chucky Michaels, and another boy. Bo Dai dropped to his knees in the grass beside him.

"You hurt? Should we call nine-one-one?"

"No, I'm OK. Thanks. Where's my brother?"

"He ran away."

"That was a UFO!" Chucky pointed out. "A real UFO!"

"I noticed," said Justin, which made the older boys laugh.

"But you didn't even act scared," said the boy whose name Justin didn't know.

"I was, though." Feeling a bit wobbly, Justin pushed himself to his feet. "Especially when he—it zapped—my library book! I'll never get it back! Mom's going to be mad. She'll never believe—"

"What book was it?"

"*Little House on the Prairie.*"

"Weird," said Chucky. "Why would they want *that*?"

"I don't know . . . maybe because it's about pioneers?" Justin thought out loud. "Maybe that's what they are?"

"Yeah . . ." Bo Dai slowly agreed. "That's smart. I wouldn't have thought of that."

"It's just a—uh theory," said Justin, glad he remembered the word, and trying not to show how pleased he was by the older boys' respect. "A logical guess. Of course, I could be wrong. Maybe he just wanted something . . . to prove he'd been here."

He fingered the faceted stone in his pocket as the four of them started to walk back across the outfield toward home.

Ten years later—when he was six feet four and had taught Paul to respect him—Justin learned the alien's gift was a red diamond. He didn't want to, but he sold it, bought his mother a house, and paid for his college education. He became an astrophysicist and dreamed of traveling to other worlds.

Twenty light-years later Zebtor managed to translate the book for which he'd paid the small alien one red cessor.

While crushed to learn his religious theory was completely wrong, he was smart enough to know a good story when he saw one. He published the book as children's science fiction about life on an alien planet. It made him so rich he never had to go into space again.

Meet the Author

H. M. Hoover was born near Alliance, Ohio. "I grew up in an old country house," she says, "with fields and woods for roaming, orchards and a pond and creeks. Pets and children were left unleashed.

"Perhaps because my parents were teachers, my finding an arrowhead washed from the sandy track of the back lane could mean learning what tribe made it, what nation the tribe belonged to, why they had fled Ohio Territory long before my father's people cleared this farm, when eagles, bears, and wolves still remained. All that led to the fact that even earlier people had lived here, hunter-gatherers following the glacier's retreat north. . . . Information kept pouring out until one almost regretted finding the arrowhead. But later I would think about it. . . ."

Ms. Hoover has lived in California and New York City and traveled extensively in the United States and parts of Europe, pursuing her interests in natural history, history, and archaeology. The author of sixteen highly acclaimed books—thirteen of which are young adult science fiction—she now lives and writes in northern Virginia.

⌣⟡

NOVELS BY H. M. HOOVER

Another Heaven, Another Earth	*Only Child*
Away Is a Strange Place to Be	*Orvis*
The Bell Tree	*The Rains of Eridan*
Children of Morrow	*Return to Earth*
The Dawn Palace	*The Shepherd Moon*
The Delikon	*This Time of Darkness*
The Lion's Cub	*Treasures of Morrow*
The Lost Star	*The Winds of Mars*

More About "Just a Theory"

SANDY ASHER: How important are futuristic, technological gizmos to a science fiction story—gamma ray guns and teletransporters and such?

H. M. HOOVER: Technology shouldn't be vital to a good science fiction story and, if counted on too much, can be a detriment since it so quickly becomes obsolete and dates the story. What makes good science fiction is the same thing that makes any good fiction—good characters and a believable plot. And good writing helps.

SA: How do you make your alien characters seem convincing to the reader?

HMH: Any character, human or alien, must be believable to the reader—and thus must have some human characteristics, be it intelligence, fear, compassion, grief, or whatever. A thorn in an alien tentacle is just as painful as a thorn in a finger or paw, for example. And to build character, it is always the small details that matter, that make the creature come alive.

SA: What does "Just a Theory" have in common with your novels for young readers?

HMH: Humor, I hope. And intelligent alien life-forms. For creatures to take the time to visit a small planet of a minor solar system at the far edge of a small galaxy, they would have to be intelligent and have a great sense of curiosity.

SA: What books—your own and others'—would you recommend to sci-fi fans?

HMH: Of my books, I'd recommend *The Lost Star, Orvis, Children of Morrow, Only Child, Away Is a Strange Place to Be,* etc. Of other writers, Mary Haynes's *Wordchanger,* Sherri Teppler's *Beauty,* William Sleator's *Interstellar Pig,* etc. There is a wealth of good SF and fantasy books any good librarian can and will recommend.

SA: Anything else you'd like to tell us about this story in particular or science fiction in general?

HMH: This sort of story is the literary equivalent of popcorn; light and meant to be enjoyed for the moment. But a truly good science fiction tale, like any good book, can alter the way we see the world to a greater or lesser degree. It can make us think, expand our sense of wonder. I started writing science fiction for children because that was the sort of story I liked best when I was young. And when well done, it is still the kind of story I like best.

10. HORROR

THERE ARE fantasies we wish would come true, and there are fantasies we hope *never* come true. *Horror stories* definitely fall into that second category. Like wild roller-coaster rides, they put us about as close to real peril as we care to go. And also like wild roller-coaster rides, they're fun because we can keep reassuring ourselves, even while our hair stands on end, that what's happening isn't nearly as dangerous as it seems. It's only a ride. It's just a story.

The closer a story comes to seeming real, the better the thrills and chills. And the deliciously creepy feelings linger longer when a horror story ends with a touch of mystery, leaving the reader to puzzle over tantalizing "whys" and "hows" and "what ifs."

Marion Dane Bauer, author of "The Wall," has this to say: "I think horror stories must begin with a strong sense of reality, even ordinariness, which draws readers in, calls up that 'willing suspension of disbelief' that all good stories demand. And if they move from there into the impossible, as they so often do, then they allow us a satisfying shiver while leaving our own world intact. There is something about being frightened in the safety of our armchairs that purges us of fear, that perhaps even brings us back with more courage to face our own all-too-real horrors."

Perhaps "The Wall" will have this effect on you. If, of course, you come back . . .

The Wall

MARION DANE BAUER

Sara twirled in the middle of her bedroom floor and dropped onto her bed. Uncle Rick was coming! And he was bringing a surprise! He had called that very morning to say he was on his way.

He had also said, "You and your mom be ready by six. I'll take you out to one of those fancy restaurants you both like so much. How about that?"

Sara reached out a hand to touch the wall next to her bed. It was solid, cool, and the flowers in the wallpaper glowed in the late-afternoon light. "Uncle Rick is coming!" she told the wall.

And then she smiled at herself for talking to a wall. Long ago, when she was quite small, she had been afraid of the inky blackness the wall next to her bed dissolved into at night.

Her usually understanding mother said, *Don't be silly, Sara. There's nothing there but a wall. See?* And indeed, when she turned on the light, Sara's flowered wall appeared, every time. But the instant the light was out, it disappeared again. And when her mother left the room, Sara always lay perfectly still, afraid to move, afraid even to cry out. The dark seemed to suck at her, to pull her, to lure her even.

Sometimes, all those long years ago, Sara had even cried for her daddy, had begged for him to come and save her. She had cried without sound, though, because her mother wouldn't have wanted to hear those tears. Her father had been swallowed up in some other darkness, and neither Sara nor her mother had seen him for a very long time.

Then Uncle Rick had come to visit, as he did now and then. And that evening it had been he who had tucked Sara into bed. When he'd turned out the light and she'd felt herself disappearing in the sudden blackness, she'd cried, "Uncle Rick! Help!" And she'd told him about the dark, about the way it beckoned.

He'd said, "But didn't you know? That's just the playground calling!" And he'd told her a story about a playground that bloomed just beyond her wall's dark face.

The playground had swings that swung without being pushed and a swirling, looping slide and a merry-go-round with carved wooden ponies. One, her uncle told her, was as white as new snow and had a single black star in the middle of his forehead. His name, of course, was Star, and he was waiting for her there. Uncle Rick himself would even meet her at the playground if she liked, and they could play all through the long night . . . right in Sara's wall.

The playground could be reached only if Sara lay completely still, facing into the dark, counting her breaths. And so, as her uncle tiptoed away, that's what she did. And naturally, she went right to sleep . . . to dream of the magical playground where her favorite uncle waited for her.

Had she known it was a dream? Not the first time, certainly. But when she had tried to go there again, she discovered that the playground wasn't something to be had merely by wanting. It was a gift that came to her whenever the gift itself wanted to come. Exactly the way her uncle did.

Sara hugged herself and rolled off the bed. It had been a

long time since she had thought about the playground, probably since Uncle Rick's last visit. That must have been six months ago, at least. And of course, they didn't talk about playgrounds when he visited anymore . . . or about the dark. She was much too old for such things now.

Sometimes, though, even now, Sara lay in bed at night facing into the wall's alluring darkness, and she couldn't help but remember the long-ago playground. And her uncle Rick. And she couldn't help but feel a bit sad to be so grown up. Perhaps this time she would talk to him about the sadness.

❧

"You look nice," Sara's mother said.

"I wish I had a new dress," Sara replied.

"The dress you have looks just fine," Mom reminded her, as Sara had known she would. "And it'll be new to Uncle Rick. He doesn't usually see you dressed up." She picked up a tube of lipstick and added, "It must be some surprise he's bringing. He's never taken us out to eat before. I wonder . . ." But the doorbell chimed just then, interrupting her wondering.

"I'll get it!" Sara cried, dashing from her mother's room. But when she reached the entryway, she paused, took a deep breath, and smoothed her dress before reaching for the doorknob.

"Sara!" The voice rang out almost before the door was open.

And though Sara had prepared herself to cry, *Uncle Rick!* she didn't. In fact, she didn't say anything. Nor did she throw herself into her uncle's arms in their usual greeting, but stopped there in the doorway, staring.

Uncle Rick stood on the porch, holding a small girl against his chest. The girl must have been four years old, much too old for being carried, but she leaned against Sara's uncle's shoulder as though the spot there suited her perfectly. She had pale, champagne-colored curls, and she peered past Sara into the house.

A woman stood next to Uncle Rick, one hand looped possessively inside his elbow.

"I told you I was bringing a surprise," Uncle Rick said, his eyes dancing light, "and here they are!"

Even the fact that Sara was standing in the doorway of her own house couldn't hold off the sudden, overwhelming feeling of having walked into a place where she didn't belong.

"This is my wife, Karen," Uncle Rick explained as Mom came up behind Sara. "We just got married last week. And our daughter, Melanie."

"For heaven's sake!" Mom exclaimed. "Rick, why didn't you tell us?"

And then there was the general commotion of introductions and hellos and congratulations. Sara stood, too unnerved to move or speak.

"Sara," the woman said, thrusting a hand with vivid red claws toward Sara's middle, "I'm so glad to meet you. Rick's been telling us all about you."

All? Sara thought, giving herself over reluctantly to the handshake.

"Come in," Mom was saying. "Come in." And everyone did, including the girl, who rode into the room like a queen surveying her court.

"Melanie," the girl's mother scolded in a sugary tone

that belied her words, "it's time to get down. You're going to make Daddy tired."

"No, I won't," Melanie replied, equally sweet, but entirely unyielding. And when Uncle Rick sat on the couch, she settled herself next to him, leaving not even a breath's space between them.

The adults all began to talk at once. Sara sat down, numbly. How could he have done it? Not just married without telling them, but arrived on their doorstep with this child, expecting them all to be glad. And was he going to take Melanie to the restaurant, too?

After a few moments, Melanie climbed down off the couch and began to poke around the room. She seemed to be looking for something, but Sara couldn't imagine what.

There was a lot of boring chatter . . . about the wedding and about where Rick and Karen had met and how, when it's truly love, you know, and you don't have to wait. Sara barely listened to any of it.

Uncle Rick stood, finally, and stretched. "I think it's time, don't you?" he asked in a general kind of way.

"Yes," Mom agreed. She stood, too.

As if on cue, Melanie emerged from the hallway. "Where're we going?" she asked, her face rumpled into a frown.

"Into the car again, Punkin." It was the name he'd called Sara once, a long time ago . . . Punkin. "We're taking these fine ladies out to eat."

"Not me," Melanie said sweetly, even smiling so that she showed a row of small, bright teeth. "I'm staying here."

"But darling," the girl's mother pleaded, "Daddy's taking us to a nice restaurant."

Melanie shook her head, whipping her translucent curls back and forth. "I don't like restaurants," she said.

Uncle Rick squatted to bring himself to the little girl's level. "We can't leave you here alone. You know that."

Melanie pointed a finger at Sara. "*She'll* stay with me," she announced.

All eyes followed the aim of the finger. Even Uncle Rick stood again and looked at Sara. Was it the first time he had really looked since he'd come in?

"It's been an awfully long day for Melanie," her mother murmured.

"Sara, would you consider . . . ?" Sara's mother started to ask, but she didn't finish the question. She knew the answer. Who wouldn't?

Sara took a deep breath. *No way!* she was going to tell them.

But then Melanie's mother spoke in a tentative kind of way, looking up at Uncle Rick. "Perhaps I should be the one to stay. You've come all this way to see Sara and your sister, after all."

Sara relaxed, just for an instant, until her uncle said, "Oh no, darling. We couldn't do that. The main reason we've come is for you and my sister to have a chance to meet."

His sister, but not his niece! The omission struck Sara like a physical blow. And before she had known she was going to say anything at all, the grim words tumbled from her lips. "Never mind. I'll do it."

The instant she had spoken, she could gladly have cut out her tongue. She held her breath, waiting for Uncle Rick to refuse her offer, too. He had to refuse. Didn't he?

Instead, he turned a dazzling smile in her direction and

pulled her into a tight hug, the first since he'd arrived. "You're fantastic!" he exclaimed, and Sara forced her unwilling arms to return the embrace.

"Maybe tomorrow . . ." she offered, after he had released her and stepped back again. She left it open for him to suggest exactly what they might do tomorrow . . . just the two of them, alone.

Uncle Rick grimaced. "I'm sorry, Punkin," he began, and Sara didn't need to listen to the rest. Something about their having to leave first thing in the morning to visit Karen's family. Something more about how he would miss their special time together.

Big deal. Besides, where did he get off calling her Punkin?

"It's all right, Uncle Rick," she heard herself saying. "It's not important." And maybe, after all, it wasn't. Maybe she had outgrown her uncle, right along with outgrowing the ridiculous playground he had manufactured in her stupid wall.

The three adults gave Sara every possible kind of instruction . . . what to feed Melanie (peanut butter and honey sandwiches were one of the few things the little dear would eat), what time Melanie should go to bed (not soon enough), where she should sleep (in Sara's own bed, no less).

And when Sara had finally closed the door behind them, there was a hard knot of anger in her chest. "Would you like a peanut butter and honey sandwich?" she asked with mechanical politeness, turning to the waiting child.

Melanie shook her head. "I want to see your wall."

"My w . . . wall?" Sara stuttered, the knot growing tighter, harder. "What are you talking about?"

"You *know*," Melanie told her. "The wall by your bed."

"Why would you want to see that?"

"I wanna play in your playground."

Sara went hot, then cold. "Who told you about . . . that?" she demanded, but of course she knew.

"Daddy told us, in the car," Melanie answered. And then, when Sara didn't respond, she asked again, "Can we?"

"See my bedroom wall?"

Melanie nodded.

Sara closed her eyes for a moment, but then she shrugged, letting the girl see how little she cared. "Sure," she said. "But you're going to be disappointed." And she led the way down the hall into her bedroom.

"No, not that," Melanie declared, barely pausing to examine the flowered wall. "It has to be dark. My daddy told me."

"Then you'll have to wait, won't you?" Sara kept her voice calm, even pleasant, but she didn't look at the child.

By the time she had fed Melanie a sandwich and read her a story and found a pair of pajamas in the pink ballerina suitcase, night had settled heavily outside the house. Melanie went willingly, even eagerly to bed.

She propped her head on the pillow in an imitation of rest. "Okay," she ordered. "Turn off the light. I'm ready."

Sara paused with her hand on the switch. "You won't be scared of the dark?"

"Scared? Puh! Only *babies* are scared of the dark." It was obvious that she had heard all about Sara herself being a baby once.

Sara flipped off the switch, and night crowded into the room, gathering thickly in the wall beside the bed. "Okay," she said, a plan beginning to form, "I'll tell you about the playground now."

"You don't have to," Melanie interrupted. "Daddy's told me everything. I'm going to ride on the white pony with the black star on his nose."

"On his forehead," Sara corrected, automatically, though she was finding it difficult to speak. Was there nothing Uncle Rick had left out?

"No," Melanie insisted. "On his nose. And he's got black stockings, too."

No, he doesn't, Sara thought, but she didn't bother to say anything more.

"And when he runs," Melanie was saying, "he runs faster than the wind."

"But he's not—" Sara stopped. *He's not alive,* she was going to say. At least, Uncle Rick had never made him alive for her. There was no use in explaining that, though, because obviously he had now.

"How about the swings?" Sara said instead. "Do you want to go on the swings . . . or the sliding board that twists around and around?"

"No." Even in the unfamiliar darkness Melanie's *no* was as solid as a rock. "I'm just going to ride Star."

Hearing the name, Sara jerked, involuntarily. So he had given away her pony's name as well! But still she asked softly, moving toward the door, "And you're sure you won't be afraid?"

"I *told* you. I'm not scared of the dark."

"Well, that's all right then," Sara said. And she added, sweetly, innocently, "I suppose you won't be afraid of a were-wolf then."

"What wolf?" Melanie's voice was thinner, younger than it had been only a moment before.

"A werewolf," Sara repeated, smiling to herself in the concealing dark. "You know. It's a man who turns into a wolf at night."

There was a brief silence, then Melanie asked, obviously working to sound unconcerned, "What does he do? The werewolf. Why does he come to your playground?"

Because I've just invited him, Sara thought, suppressing a giggle, but out loud she said, "He doesn't do much. Just eats little girls. But I'm sure you're not afraid."

"No," Melanie agreed, though her voice wavered this time. "I'm not afraid. Anyway, my daddy will be there. Won't he?"

"Oh, yes," Sara assured her. "Your daddy will be there." And then she didn't say anything more. Just stood there. Just waited.

"My daddy's bigger than any werewolf. Stronger, too."

"He's big and strong all right," Sara said. "But . . ." She let her voice trail off, as though she couldn't force herself to say the terrible words.

"What?" Melanie demanded.

"Didn't he tell you?" Sara's voice dripped sympathy. She was reaching for the door handle as she spoke. "He's the one. When he gets to the playground at night, he turns into a werewolf. Every time."

"My daddy?" The breath seemed to have been squeezed from Melanie's chest.

"Listen!" Sara commanded. "Can't you hear him? He's laughing. At you and me, I suppose."

In the deep silence, she could feel the little girl listening.

Sara slipped into the hall, closing the door behind her.

~&

It had been half an hour, maybe more, since she left Melanie. She'd done a terrible thing. She knew that.

The silence that followed her exit astonished her, annoyed her, too. She meant to go right back in. She would have if Melanie had cried, even if she had called out once. But the little girl hadn't made a sound, and Sara hadn't been able to force herself to return to retract her story.

She stood up and flipped the TV off. Maybe she should go check, just once.

She moved through the shadowy hall and opened the bedroom door. The dim light from the window played on the rumpled covers, illuminating the bed faintly without penetrating the blackness of the wall. As always.

Sara tiptoed to the side of the bed and stopped there, waiting for her eyes to adjust to the darkness so she could make out the shape of the child. If Melanie wasn't asleep, she would tell her that her daddy wasn't a werewolf, that there was no such thing as werewolves, really. But Sara couldn't quite make out the girl's small shape in the bed.

"Melanie?" she whispered, patting the flat surface of the mattress. "Melanie!"

It was then that she heard the laughter for the first time . . . gay, playful. Uncle Rick! And the answering trill must be Melanie. Who else could it be? Unless it was a pony's whinny.

Sara stepped toward the wall, her heart hammering. "Uncle Rick?" she called, though she felt foolish speaking. Uncle Rick was at the restaurant. She had seen him leave, and he hadn't yet returned. She knew that.

The laughter came again, higher this time, fiercer, and Sara's knees went soft. She lifted one trembling hand to support herself against the wall. But her hand found no support. No wall. There was only the impenetrable darkness, which gave way suddenly, dissolving into space before her touch. And the next thing Sara knew, she was falling.

"Uncle Rick!" she gasped, twisting, reaching for something solid, for light and hope.

But there was nothing. Not even a playground. Not even a white pony. Only the endless descent. And the laughter. The cruel, cruel laughter.

Meet the Author

"I have been writing stories for kids for more than twenty years," says Marion Dane Bauer, "and I still love doing it. The best known of my books and the one most frequently used in classrooms is *On My Honor,* which won a Newbery Honor Award in 1987. And lately I've begun to turn my hand to picture books (the texts, not the pictures) and to a couple of easy readers and even to a bit of poetry. What I like about those kinds of shorter pieces is the opportunity they give me to play with words. I believe that a simple love of words lies at the base of every writer's career. And the love of a good story comes very close after."

BOOKS BY MARION DANE BAUER

NOVELS

A Dream of Queens and Castles	*Like Mother, Like Daughter*
Face to Face	*On My Honor*
Foster Child	*A Question of Trust*
Ghost Eye	*Rain of Fire*

| *Shelter from the Wind* | *A Taste of Smoke* |
| *Tangled Butterfly* | *Touch the Moon* |

NONFICTION
What's Your Story? A Young Person's Guide to Writing Fiction
A Writer's Story, From Life to Fiction

ANTHOLOGY
Am I Blue? Coming Out from the Silence (editor and
    contributor)

PICTURE BOOK
When I Go Camping with Grandma

EASY READER
Alison's Wings

❧

More About "The Wall"

MARION DANE BAUER: When I was a young child, I was terribly afraid of the black of the night wall beside my bed, and I always slept turned on my side to face the pale light from the window on the other side of the room. In those early years my brother and I shared a bedroom in our small, four-room house, and one night we continued talking across the room long after we were supposed to be asleep. Mother finally ordered us to turn toward our respective walls and to stay that way. I was terrified to face the wall, but I did and fell asleep . . . and dreamed.

In the dream, an old man sat high in a wagon, driving a pair of dappled gray horses. (The man was not a product of my imagination. A farmer outside of our small Illinois town still farmed with a pair of big, gray work horses well into the forties and used them, as well, to pull a wagon into town.) In my dream, however, man and horses and wagon came in through my bedroom window, drove around the wall behind my brother's bed, and out into the middle of the floor.

The wagon was filled with children. "Come on, Marion," they called, and I climbed out of my bed and into the wagon. Then the man drove the dappled horses into the impenetrable black of my night wall . . . where a playground waited. The children and I played all night long, only returning to the wagon when the old man called. Then he drove out of the wall and around my bed. "Good-bye, Marion," the children called, and I climbed out of the wagon and back into bed. And then it was morning.

I think I knew, even then, that the old man and the dappled horses and the children and the playground were part of a dream, but the dream was so real that I'm not entirely sure I did. I do know that, night after night, I forced myself to go to sleep facing the black of my wall, hoping they would come again. And sometimes they did.

Several times over the years I have used that dream as the basis for a story. In this version, I didn't set out intending to write a horror story. The horror just crept up on me. And once it was there, I decided to let it stay. My memories, however, of that playground in the night wall are still very dear. They may find their way to another story yet.

SANDY ASHER: Is "The Wall" similar to other things you've written?

MDB: I have written a number of ghost stories, but "The Wall" is the only horror story that has ever come to me. And yet there is much about "The Wall" that will feel very familiar to those who know my work. My stories always center around relationship issues, usually relationships inside families, often the relationship between a child and parent figure. And my stories always move toward a strong climax, sometimes a climax that centers around an actual or possible death. The only real difference between this story and the rest of my work is that "The Wall" offers no resolution, which means that it carries no serious meaning. Is Sara being punished for her cruelty to Melanie? Perhaps. If so, who or what is punishing her? Who knows?

SA: Can you recommend books of your own and other authors to readers who enjoy this genre?

MDB: Joan Aiken comes immediately to mind. She can set off shivers with the best. Of my own work, the novel *A Taste of Smoke* is a ghost story, if one with a gentler outcome than "The Wall." And I am currently gathering the various ghost stories I have written to be published together as a book. So you can watch for that.

11. FOLKTALE

*F*OLKTALES may differ from culture to culture, and even within one culture's literary tradition. Some folktales are light and humorous; others quite dark and violent. There are those with magical elements: glass mountains, wishes that come true just for the asking, giants, trolls, leprechauns, and ghosts. And there are those that seem *almost* realistic, such as the tales told about legendary heroes that perhaps stretch the truth just a bit—or a lot!

Folktales may be about animals that speak or princesses who don't. But what they all have in common is that they've been passed from generation to generation orally—as spoken stories—before being written down. Traveling through hundreds of years and across thousands of miles, they carry with them valued traditions and folk wisdom.

Like all the storytellers that came before them, modern writers find ways for their audiences to enjoy these stories as if they were brand new. In "A Sheepish Answer," a folktale retold by Carol Kendall and Yao-wen Li, the fifth century Chinese characters and their problems and concerns seem quite familiar. So does the story's sense of humor.

A Sheepish Answer

Carol Kendall
and Yao-wen Li

In a village tucked away in the folds of China there once lived a scholar and his wife who were happy and content enough in the way of families until the wife fell prey to the terrible pangs of jealousy.

Although her husband spent most of his waking hours, and even some of his sleeping hours, at his writing table, she could not get it out of her head that he was casting sheep's eyes at his neighbor's daughters. No matter how often he disclaimed an interest in anybody beyond his own fine family or how often the rest of the family defended him, when the scholar stepped out of the door into the garden, his wife cursed him roundly. Dared he put a foot into the road to walk about the village, she rushed after him and pounded his back with her fists, uttering dire threats.

The scholar, a mild man who only wanted peace and the opportunity to pursue his writing, put up with the jagged edge of his wife's tongue and the fistfuls of blows she dealt him until she went beyond all bounds and tied a long rope round one of his legs. Should he linger in the courtyard privy more than a few moments, twitch! went the rope, and he was hauled back into the house. She even kept him on a lead while he worked at his writing table, twitching him to her whenever she thought his mind might be straying from his books.

So great were her demands on him that even he, the meekest of scholars, knew that he must set himself free from her terrible tyranny. The opportunity came one day when, as he stood hobbled at the gate while his wife, worn out from her scolding, had gone soundly to sleep, the local sorceress passed by.

"Szzzt," said the scholar of a sudden, surprising himself as much as the sorceress. "Help me!" He glanced nervously toward the house. "You see my condition. If I were to take this rope from my leg to go walking about the town, my wife would know it in an instant and come after me. What can I do? My life is intolerable!"

With that the rope gave a wriggle and then a yank, and the scholar almost went sprawling.

"I come, I come," he called to his wife, but turned pleading eyes to the sorceress.

"Tomorrow, same time," the sorceress whispered. "I'll consider your plight."

"Who is that you are talking to?" cried the wife. "Come in here!" and she jerked the rope so vigorously that the scholar went catty-winkle and measured his length across the doorsill. "Can't I even close my eyes for one moment without your carrying on with the first woman who prances by?"

"T'was but the sorceress, dear one," said the scholar. "It were well to stay friends with the sorceress, my heart. I asked her to give me an enduring love charm that will bind us together forever."

"Ah then," said his wife, mollified for the moment. "If I could only be sure of you always . . . Come, get off the ground and let me untie the rope from your dear foot."

But the next day, all of the old jealousies surged through her anew, and the rope was back around the scholar's leg as tightly as ever. It took all of his blandishments and "dear hearts" to get her to lie down for her usual midday nap, but at last her light snore signaled that she was asleep, and the scholar edged carefully out the door to meet the sorceress. . . .

❧

The wife woke with a start when the rope, wrapped once round her wrist, gave a sharp tug.

"Ho, then!" she cried. "I know what you are up to, husband! A body can't so much as take twenty blinks in peace. Come in here, Master Scholar!" She gave a yank at the rope.

"Baa-a-aaaa."

"What's that you're saying to me? What are you then, a sheep to make a bleating like that!" She yanked again.

"Baaa-a-aaa-aaaaaa."

Infuriated at such disrespect from her husband, she pulled and tugged at the rope until she hauled him through the door. . . .

"Baa-aaaa-aaa," he bleated.

Merciful goddess, he had turned into a sheep!

The wailings! The lamentings! The wife summoned the children large and small, aunts and uncles young and old, the grandparents from both sides, to see this pitiable condition of her husband.

"O mercy upon us!" she cried, throwing her arms about the sheep and holding him close. "How has this come to pass? O my beloved husband, turn back into your dearly treasured self once more!"

The sheep made no sign of turning into a scholar, dearly

treasured or otherwise. He stood and chewed and chewed and looked at the wife with his gold-barred eyes until, in confusion and fright, she threw a shawl over her head and ran out to fetch the sorceress.

That artful woman came at once and when she had heard the wife's piteous tale from beginning to end, she nodded her head wisely. "Indeed, this is a case that I have had some experience with," she said. "Your husband's condition was brought on by your own scolding mouth and your fisted hand. It is a punishment visited upon you by your ancestors for your jealousy and can be reversed only if you truly repent and change your wicked ways."

"O I shall! I promise!" wailed the wife, gathering the sheep affectionately into her arms. "I swear it, dear husband." She lifted her tear-soaked face to the sorceress. "Only tell me what to do."

"Very well," said the sorceress briskly. "You must of course untie that wretched rope from your husband's leg and set him free to roam as he will."

"Done!" cried the wife, releasing the sheep at once.

"For your repentance," the sorceress went on, "you must give up wine and meat for seven days. Boiled water and thin cabbage will sustain you and clear your mind of wickedness."

"Done!"

"Further, the entire family gathered here, young and old, large and small, thick and thin, must remain inside the house and speak to no one outside it. This, for the space of seven days."

"Done! Done! Done!"

"Further, and last, you must worship the gods and beg them to transform the sheep back into your husband. If you obey all of these instructions down to the last cabbage leaf, I have no doubt that your husband will be restored to you in his more usual shape."

"I promise to do all and everything you say!" cried the wife, fresh tears of penitence already soaking the front of her gown.

While the sheep trailed out of the gate behind the sorcer-- ess, the wife gathered together the rest of the family, tall, short, thick and thin, young and old, and urged them inside the house, fastening the doors and windows tight so that there could be no accidental straying outside. And there they stayed for seven days while the wife rigidly observed the fast and prayed hourly that the gods would restore her husband to his true and beloved self.

So it was that at the end of the seventh day, to the hour, they heard a bleating outside.

The wife burst into new lamentations. "O goddess of mercy, am I then to be doomed forever to the bleating of a sheep? Haven't I done all the duties the sorceress ordered, well and truly? Haven't I—" She stopped short. "Did I hear the sound of the gate just now?" She turned toward the door- way, not quite daring to hope. . . .

The door opened, and the scholar, hands in sleeves and a faint smile shaping his lips, walked in.

It took some time for the excitement to die down. A feast was got ready with all the scholar's favorite foods spread out on the table, and everybody pushed and shoved everybody else to serve the returned one.

At last the wife burst out, "But what was it like being a sheep? Did you not suffer? In spite of our loving kindness toward you?"

The scholar's mouth turned down as though in memory

of his ordeal, and he rubbed his stomach with many a grimace. "Ahhh-hhhh," he groaned, "it was eating grass that was the worst. How my stomach did grumble and ache!"

"O my poor dear husband, my heart," his wife sobbed. "Never again will I show a jealous face!"

Smiling happily, her husband nodded. The next day he arose early and, before beginning work, strolled about the village—not failing to pay a courtesy call on the sorceress as he passed her house.

Ever after that, whenever jealousy's fingers laid hold of the wife, the scholar had only to drop on all fours and bleat to bring her to her senses. And so they and their family lived very happily.

And whenever the scholar saw a certain sheep grazing in the village, he winked at it. The sheep, however, just went on chewing.

—You Dong-zhi,
Tales of Jealous Women, fifth century

Meet the Authors

Carol Kendall was born in Bucyrus, Ohio, where, she says, she "lived uneventfully as the youngest child in the company of six brothers, all of whom talked rather a lot." This made her realize very early that the only way to make her voice heard was through the written word. She began her first book, a diary, when she was in first grade, but it never got past the opening line, "Today I saw my first robin." Her second book, begun in the fourth grade, grew quickly to cover eighteen pencil-written pages in a composition book. Her teacher's comment on reading it: "Don't be so silly, Carol!"

Undaunted, Carol Kendall has gone on to publish mystery novels for adults and young readers, three fantasies, and many retold folktales. When she isn't writing, she says, her "preferred activity is traveling—as far from home as possible short of going to the moon." Favorite destinations include

Tibet, Easter Island, and Iceland. "Choice stories lie hidden in places like these. In the very stones."

Yao-wen Li was born in Guangzhou, China. When she was twelve, her family moved to Hong Kong for safety during the Japanese invasion of China. After Pearl Harbor, her family was on the move again and she was sent to Chengdu, in Sichuan province, to attend Ginling College. At the end of World War II, she came to America and earned an M.S. degree from the University of Iowa. She married Chu-Tsing Li, an art historian, and they have two children.

While raising a family, Yao-wen Li worked as a research assistant in the department of surgery at the University of Iowa. After her children grew up, she became a freelance writer and has published many stories in literary magazines, as well as a book of folktales, *Sweet and Sour,* written with Carol Kendall. Much of Yao-wen Li's writing is based on her childhood memories, which she came to enjoy after her trips back to China as an adult.

BOOKS BY CAROL KENDALL

NOVELS	FOLKTALES
The Firelings	*Haunting Tales from Japan*
The Gammage Cup	*Sweet and Sour* (with Yao-wen Li)
The Whisper of Glocken	*The Wedding of the Rat Family*

More About "A Sheepish Answer"

CAROL KENDALL: When I began to study Chinese some thirty years ago, I immediately felt at home with the language, as I never had, quite, with Russian, German, or French, all of which I had previously studied with joy and enthusiasm. I particularly took to Chinese folktales. This is none so strange, as my own books of fantasy have a folktale flavor about them.

By the time I was fluent enough to begin translating my favorite Chinese tales into English, we had moved from Ohio to Lawrence, Kansas, where I met Yao-wen Li. She was also beginning to translate Chinese stories into English, but from a different perspective. Neither of us was a star in the other's first language, but we came together as naturally as soy sauce and ginger.

SANDY ASHER: Are there many changes in the original folktale when you retell it?

CK: Yao-wen and I agreed that our versions of the folktales should be true to the original Chinese. There would be no changes in storylines, no rewriting of endings to make them more acceptable to Westerners. Because Chinese tales are terse—skin and bone and a stray hank of hair!—translating becomes a matter of fleshing out and fattening both character and action, always in keeping with the bare plot of the original. Dialogue, if it appears, must be rendered with the ring of authenticity: "Golly!" for instance, just won't do as a substitute for the Chinese "Ai-yah!"

There is, of course, one cautionary note: When you set out to retell a story, you must never forget that you are *re*-telling it—in your own words, your own phrases, your own sentences. There is an ugly word called plagiarism that you want to avoid at all costs!

SA: What advice do you have for other writers who are interested in finding folktales worth retelling to modern readers?

CK: Finding the original folktales to translate was sometimes a pain, more for me than for Yao-wen, who can scan a table of contents printed in Chinese in short minutes, while I might spend long hours, with my thirty-two dictionaries at hand, to make sense of all the titles. But there is no dearth of English-language anthologies of folktales. On my own bookshelves I have six worldwide collections and fifty-some editions of tales from Africa, India, Iceland, Finland, Russia, France, Australia, Mexico. . . . For readers who are not avid collectors, most of these books are in local or school libraries. Go look!

For anyone interested in retelling folktales, my best advice is to read any folktales that come to hand. Sample here and there, country to country, until you find the stories that take you by the heart, about which you might say, "I almost could have written that!" Translating, of course, is different from retelling. You do not actually *have* to read or speak the original language, but you do need to have some understanding of the country and the people if you are going to retell their stories. Our rule of thumb for any tale was that we liked it: beginning, end, and middle!

12. CONTEMPORARY REALISM

"REALISM IS so personal," Angela Johnson said, way back in the first interview for this book. Indeed it is. In our final story, "An Education" by Marie G. Lee, we come full circle, back to *contemporary realism*, but we find characters and a situation very different from those in Angela Johnson's "Flying Away"—except that both authors create a realistic world that could exist right here, right now.

Each of us interprets what we see and hear in our own way, and that's what makes each writer's story unlike any other, even within the same genre. Fantasy is personal, too. Adventure stories, animal stories, horror stories—they all reflect the tastes, experiences, and imaginations of the people who write them.

In "An Education," we learn that reality can be just as personal as realism: Not only do we each see and hear real things differently, we often see and hear different things. . . .

An Education
❧ MARIE G. LEE

Helen stood on her tiptoes, straining to grasp the roll of CON-
GRATULATIONS GRADUATE! wrapping paper that she knew was
somewhere on the shelf. She had spent a lot of time on
Amanda's present—a favorite picture of the two of them sitting atop Amanda's red Mustang in front of the high school
framed in a clever wooden frame that had Minnesota loons
on the corners—and she wanted to get the wrapping just
right.

Her fingers fanned air, then touched something cool,
smooth, and leather. When she stood on top of a stool, she
could see that the wrapping paper had fallen to the back of
the shelf, and underneath the ribbons and paper was a thin,
ugly scrapbook with a leatherette cover.

She ran her fingers along the cheap gilt border stamped
on the cover. She couldn't believe that her tasteful parents
would buy something like this.

Squares of light blue tissue paper fluttered out from behind the cover as she stood on the stool. She jumped to the
floor and stooped to pick one up. It was an airmail letter, the
kind you wrote on a single sheet of blue and later folded up
neatly into an envelope. The entire letter, inside and out,
was written in Korean—she knew only because she remembered how the characters looked like squashed bugs.

Helen stared and stared at the writing, hoping perhaps
that some kind of vestigial Korean memory stuck in her

genes would let her decipher it. Were these characters letters, or were they supposed to form pictures, like they do in Chinese? No matter how she looked at them, they didn't look like anything to her.

"If I'm Korean," she had once said to her parents, "then why won't you teach me to read and write Korean?"

"You're American," her mother had said. "You don't need to waste your time on that old stuff. Spend time on your homework."

"Listen to your mother," her father had agreed.

She didn't argue with her parents, but she wanted to know more. She was just as "American" as anyone in Brainerd, so she hated it when kids teased her about her looks. She wasn't ugly, she just wasn't Caucasian like they all were; they made it seem like being Korean was something to be ashamed of—and if her parents wouldn't defend it, she almost believed it was.

"Don't listen to those kids," Amanda had said the day one of the flannel-shirted bullies in their class had come up to her and stretched his eyes into slits with his hands and grinned a bucktooth grin.

"Ah-so," he'd said, and all his friends had laughed like it was the funniest joke in the world.

She'd remembered thinking of nothing else besides running to her boyfriend's house, grabbing his hunting rifle, and mowing all those creeps down. Then, she would never go to college, but would die happy in jail.

"They're just jealous," Amanda had explained. "You're so much smarter than they are."

But she didn't feel smart. She just felt Korean and didn't know if it was a good feeling.

She carefully turned the page of the scrapbook. A yellowed newspaper clipping, her parents' wedding announcement from the *Brainerd Tribune,* stared back at her. Her father, it said, was from some Pusan province of Korea. Her mother was from somewhere called Taegu. Yet her father was wearing a tux and her mother a white dress as if it were the most natural thing in the world to do. Helen imagined that traditional Korean wedding garb was in vivid colors, not the boring black-and-white Western stuff.

She then came across a page with a black-and-white photo stuck somewhat crookedly on it. It was of a young Korean woman in a striped gown (much like the one she imagined they'd used for weddings) holding a smiling moon-faced boy. The little boy's hair was short and sea-urchin straight, and stuck up on top of his head.

On this page, there was also a glossy piece of paper caught in the binding. Helen took it out. On one side, a woman in an old-fashioned pointy bra said "For fresher taste, smoke . . ." Here the words captured in a bubble rising from her mouth were torn away. The other side was just a block of pink color.

Helen considered not bothering to put the scrap back, but in the end, she did. If anything, it was torn into such a nice, neat square.

The rest of the pages were all blank. In all, a pretty uninteresting book.

She carefully returned it to its place on the wrapping paper shelf, piled all sorts of papers and ribbons on top of it, and resumed preparing her friend's present. They were both going to be college girls this fall.

On graduation night, the two friends exchanged presents. Amanda had gotten Helen a beautiful silver necklace with a small charm on it that had Amanda's initials, A.S., on one side, and her own, H.K., on the other.

"It's so you'll remember me when you're in college way out East," Amanda said.

"Amanda, you're always so creative with presents," Helen said, reverently holding the necklace up to the light, then putting it around her neck.

She handed Amanda her present.

"Oh," Amanda said, her eyes lighting up when she saw the picture. "This is so perfect. And I love the frame."

Arm in arm, the two girls strode off to the school's auditorium, where they were going to graduate.

The friends had to separate to get into the alphabetic order of the line. The students were rustling restlessly as they waited in the halls outside the auditorium, like cattle before a stampede.

Finally, the strains of "Pomp and Circumstance" were heard, and the students shuffled out, making their way toward the stage. Helen looked into the audience for her parents, but it was too dark to see.

Mr. Oleson, the principal, stood in the middle of the stage with the diplomas, and Mr. Maki, the assistant principal, was at the far end of the stage and would be calling the names.

This was Mr. Maki's first year as an assistant principal, so he had never done a graduation before. He nervously transferred the list of names from one hand to the other. When he finally started to speak, his voice shook.

"Karen Adams," he said, too fast. "Brad Ahola, Paul Bonelli, Julie Christiansen."

Graduates clustered around Mr. Oleson as he handed out the diplomas. He stopped to frown at Mr. Maki, who blushed and tried to call the names more slowly.

"Helen Kim," Mr. Maki said, finally. Helen stepped briskly into the light of the stage amidst the sounds of clapping for the person who'd gone ahead of her.

"Chink!" hissed a voice from the line of kids.

Her feet froze. She looked out into the dark audience, but there was no one there to help her.

"Karen Lang," said Mr. Maki, and by some miracle, Helen's feet lifted and started to move again. She had no idea how long she'd been petrified like that. Seconds? Minutes? Years. Now, what were her parents going to think?

"Congratulations," Mr. Oleson said, handing her a diploma. As if in a fuzzy dream, Helen shook his hand, smiled, and calmly walked off the stage.

After the ceremony, Helen bumped into Amanda.

"We're graduated now, sweetie," Amanda said, giving her friend a hug.

"Mandy, did you hear what someone said when I went to get my diploma?"

Her friend looked blank.

"What do you mean?"

Just then, her boyfriend, Karl, came up to her and brushed her long black hair away from her face to kiss her. She looked from Amanda's puzzled face to Karl's.

"Karl, did you hear anything funny when I went up to get my diploma?" she asked.

Karl's look mirrored Amanda's.

"Anything funny?" he said. "Did Maki say your name wrong or something?"

"No, no," she said, taking off her mortar board. The tassel swung back and forth like a hypnotist's pendulum. "I think I must have imagined it."

Outside, all the parents were waiting to take pictures. Helen posed with Amanda, then Karl, then both. Her mother stood by smiling while her father snapped frame after frame.

I must have imagined it, she thought, because no one is upset.

Satisfied, she went back to Amanda's house where the two changed their clothes and then went out for a night of graduation parties.

When Helen finally returned home, it was well past midnight. She had never stayed out so late before.

There was a single light on in the kitchen, and her father sat under it, the ugly scrapbook she had found open in front of him.

"Uh, hello, Dad," she said, as she started to make her way up the stairs. Her father looked so still, so strange sitting there under that pyramid of light.

"What happened to you tonight made me think of this book," he said.

Her foot froze on the stair.

Her father gave her a gentle smile, which drew her back to the kitchen table.

"What is this?" she said.

"It's a book of the few memories I brought with me from Korea," he said, smoothing a worn page with his slender surgeon's fingers. "I was hoping I wouldn't have to bring it out again."

"What do you mean?"

"When you leave a country," he said, "it is like an animal caught in a trap that gnaws a limb off to free itself. You can't dwell on what you have left behind—if you want to survive. You have to go on with what you have."

"Yes," Helen said, even though she wasn't sure she understood.

"When your mother and I came to this country, we were not ready for the way we would be treated. People shouted at us and called us Chinese—or even Japanese!—or just made it clear that they did not like our yellow skin. Look how tonight someone thought you were Chinese.

"When I was a little boy in Korea," he went on, "I used to stand for hours outside the U.S. Embassy in order to get a view of these mysterious creatures, the Americans. They were always so loud and happy—they fascinated me. When I was at the university, the American GIs in Seoul would give us magazines that they were going to throw away. My favorite one was *Life*. I liked the pictures, and the colors—more vivid and beautiful than anything you could find in an ancient Korean volume—and here were these people throwing these magazines away. I thought America had to be a special place if you could do that."

"Especially wasteful," Helen said, but her father appeared not to hear her.

"So one day when I came across the most beautiful rose color," he said, resting his elbows on the table and rubbing his eyes under his glasses, "more beautiful than any flower I ever got for your mother—I saved it and put it up in my little locker to inspire me to study hard—especially English. From that moment I knew I was going to go to America—to *Life*."

Helen did not know what to say. She felt her throat was stopped up.

"So, although America was not quite as I expected," her father said, "I have always hoped it would be better for you." He played with the corner of one of the blue letters lying on the table.

"But I see now that an American upbringing does not erase the differences of your skin and eyes." He gently touched the back of her hand. It made her shiver.

Helen cleared her throat and said, "I should like to learn Korean."

Her father looked at her, then slowly smiled. He turned the page of the book. The photo of the young woman and the moon-faced boy looked back at her, and the pink paper lay wedged in the binding.

"Mama," her father said, putting his finger lightly on the photo. "Omoni."

"Omoni," Helen repeated softly.

Meet the Author

A second-generation Korean-American, Marie G. Lee was born and raised in Hibbing, Minnesota. "Many books influenced me when I was young," she says. "Books by Judy Blume and S. E. Hinton totally shocked me because they were so honest and *real*. Another book I loved was *One Fat Summer* by Robert Lipsyte. It's about a boy who's overweight and how he learns to deal with different pressures in his life. I've never been a boy and I've never been overweight, but that book seemed so amazingly real to me that I can still quote parts of it even though I read it when I was twelve."

Along with her highly praised books for young readers, Ms. Lee has published many articles and stories in anthologies, periodicals, and literary journals.

NOVELS BY MARIE G. LEE

Finding My Voice   *Necessary Roughness*
If It Hadn't Been for Yoon Jun   *Saying Goodbye*

More About "An Education"

MARIE G. LEE: I was looking through my high school year-book and thinking about how bittersweet graduation night was. My graduation was actually pretty ordinary: my friends and I got our diplomas and partied all night. I think this story takes the bittersweet emotions I was feeling and makes them into something concrete. Now, when I look at the story, I see that the two nights—the one I had and the one the character had—are completely different action-wise, yet emotionally, they're very similar.

SANDY ASHER: How do you anchor your characters in what appears to be a real world?

MGL: Dialogue is the number-one thing. I try to relax and let the characters speak in their own words, even if I don't like the way they talk. Sometimes, characters use profanity and/or bad grammar, which I don't approve of, but if that's how they talk, that's how they talk. Number two is the characters' sensory reactions to their surroundings. When I write, I am actually in the world with my characters. I see what they see, smell what they smell, and try to incorporate that into the story.

SA: Ordinary events take on dramatic significance in your story: a scrapbook found in a closet, graduation day, a conversation between father and daughter. What advice do you have for other writers looking for the stories hidden in their day-to-day experiences?

MGL: Lots of times, you don't even know you have a story until you get it down on paper. I'll just write something but have no idea why I'm doing it. But once it's down on paper, I can pick out things and think, "Hey! There's a story in here." Life doesn't follow a narrative pattern, so creating a story often involves writing a bunch of stuff down and then picking out the unusual or significant parts.

SA: You've told me that this story is similar, but not identical, to a scene in your novel *Finding My Voice*. How does the short story differ from the novel?

MGL: A short story has to compress a lot of things into a few pages, and in the novel I had ample time to build up a whole story line of the protagonist not getting along with her father, and then the graduation night scene served as an opportunity to get to know her father better.

SA: So you would recommend *Finding My Voice* to readers who enjoy "An Education" and contemporary realism in general.

MGL: Definitely. And its sequel, *Saying Goodbye*, because I've gotten letters from readers saying it's "very real," and I even had a friend who went through many of the same things my character goes through, and he kept saying things like "How did you know how that felt?" which made me feel good as a writer, sort of like I'd done my job.

READ ON . . .

I've classified these stories by genre to emphasize how many different kinds of stories there are, but classifications can be tricky. There *is* a sheep in "A Sheepish Answer," and a rhinoceros in "A Time to Stand Up," but you probably wouldn't call either of those an animal story. Why not? Because unlike Tug the mule in "Tug, in His Own Time," the sheep and rhinoceros aren't the main focus of the stories in which they appear.

The most significant elements of a story decide its genre. But not all stories fit neatly into one category. And even with eleven different genres, this book hasn't covered all of the possibilities.

The alien encounter in "Just a Theory" is far more central to the plot than the softball game, so it makes more sense to call it "science fiction" than a "sports story."

But that means there was no example of the *sports story* genre in this book.

And, as you no doubt noticed, there was a glimpse of a ghost in "Echoes Down the Rails," but it wasn't really a ghost story. So you'll have to look elsewhere for an example of the *ghost story* genre as well. And for genres not even mentioned here. And for stories that don't fit into one particular genre . . .

That's the point! Reading fiction is like finding a treasure chest with no bottom to it. No matter how deeply you dig, there will always be more wonderful surprises. There are no limits—not in the stories available, not in the imaginations of writers creating new stories every day, and not in the delights that await us as readers. So I hope you'll go treasure hunting and discover more stories—all kinds of stories—for yourself.

You may even want to add your own writing to the treasure chest. There's plenty of room.

Ah! But that's *another* story!